His Proposed Deal

Sandi Lynn

Sandi Lynn

His Proposed Deal

Copyright © 2015 Sandi Lynn

Cover Design by Cassy Roop @ Pink Ink Designs

Photography by Sara Eirew @ Sara Eirew Photography

Models: Michel Giroux Fashion & Fitness Model and Tanya

Editing by B.Z. Hercules

Table of Contents

Chapter 1

I finished putting the last loose curl in my long, blonde hair when Kara walked into the bathroom.

"I can't believe you're leaving in the morning."

"I know. I'm going to miss you guys."

I ran my fingers through my hair and swept a bit more mascara on the lashes around my blue eyes before Kara and I headed to meet the girls for dinner. It was our last dinner together in Florida before I hopped on a plane to New York City tomorrow. I would be attending the fall semester at Parsons School of Design. It had been a dream of mine since I was a child. I worked as a waitress in an upscale restaurant and saved all my tips and a good chunk of my paychecks for over a year to be able to move to New York and live for a while until I found a job. With the help of a student loan I was able to secure, tuition wasn't a problem.

Kara and I met our friends, Molly and Aubrey, at Seafood Haven, and then we were off to a club. The four of us had been best friends since elementary school when we were put in a group together for a project. Kara and Molly were hairdressers and worked at the same salon, and Aubrey was on her way to becoming a lawyer. My dream had always been interior design and, at the age of twenty-four, I was finally pursuing it. Life hadn't been so easy for me and my mom. My dad took off when I was two and my mom always struggled to make ends meet. When she'd work double shifts at the diner, my Aunt Laura would look after me. My mom did her best, and as soon as I was old enough to work, I got a job. After graduating high school, I put off college so I could work full-time and help my mom with the bills.

"So have you talked to Justin at all?" Kara asked.

"No. He doesn't know that I'm leaving and I want to keep it that way. So don't any one of you go and tell him."

"It's too bad things didn't work out between you two," Molly spoke.

"Yeah. He's a nice guy but way too boring. I mean, come on; we never went out because he couldn't tear himself away from his video games. Not to mention the fact that he refused job offers because he felt like they weren't good enough. He has a lot of growing up to do."

"But the sex was good, right?" Aubrey asked.

"Yeah. That was the only thing that was right with our relationship. I put up with his shenanigans for a year and I just couldn't take it anymore."

"But he cried when you broke it off with him." Kara smirked.

"He cried because I broke the X-Box game he was playing when I was trying to break up with him and he wouldn't listen to me. I'm done with guys unless they're over the age of thirty-five. Hopefully, they'll have their shit figured out by then."

We all laughed, paid our bill, and headed to Club Fifty-Seven.

****

I was standing with my back leaning up against the bar, sipping a mojito and watching the girls twerking on the dance floor when a ruggedly handsome gentleman walked up and ordered a scotch on the rocks. I studied his six-foot stature as he talked to his friend. His light brown short hair was styled to perfection, as was the stubble and light mustache he sported. He wore a pair of black jeans – at least they looked black in the dim light – with a button-down short-sleeve black shirt. I gulped when he turned my way and caught me staring at him. His lips were full and his gray eyes caught my attention faster than the rest of him did. He gave me a small smile.

"Hello."

I nodded as I held up my mojito, feeling like a complete ass for getting caught. The bartender handed him his drink and he stepped closer to me.

"I'm Max."

"Emma. Nice to meet you." I smiled.

"Nice to meet you too, Emma. Want to go somewhere and talk?"

That was code for "Let's go fuck somewhere and call it a night."

"Sorry. I'm with my friends."

"Your friends can join too." He winked. His wink made him even sexier than he already was.

"You're cute but I'm not into that."

He leaned closer to me until his lips were dangerously close to mine. The smell of scotch on his breath swept over my face.

"I would love to know what you're into." His smile distracted me from my thoughts for a moment.

"I bet you would." My finger ran down the front of his shirt. "I bet you say that to all the girls."

"Only the ones I find incredibly sexy. And judging from my hard-on, you're one sexy girl."

My body was overheating as I signaled for the bartender to get me another mojito. Max threw down some cash as the bartender handed me my drink.

"It's on me."

"So now you expect sex because you bought me a drink?" I smirked as I took a sip. "I'm not that kind of girl."

His finger slowly traced the outline of my jaw as he tilted his head and stared into my eyes. "Why don't you tell me what kind of girl you are?"

This game was pretty fun. But then again, what if he was some psychotic killer that was going to stalk me and murder me for turning him down.

"I'm the type of girl who doesn't have sex with strangers. Especially those from a club. I like to get to know my men before I take them to bed. A few dates, some flowers, amazing dinners, and most importantly, the finest chocolates money can buy."

"Well, I'm sorry that I won't be able to do that for you because I'm flying out tomorrow morning. So, why don't you live life on the edge and forget all that stuff for once, and we can get straight to the bed part."

I certainly couldn't fault the poor guy for trying. My panties were wet. That hadn't happened in a very long time. Not even with Justin. But nonetheless, no matter how horny I was at this moment, I couldn't have sex with this incredibly hot and sexy man standing in front of me. It wasn't me and I wasn't about to do anything stupid for my own sexual satisfaction. Molly, Kara, and Aubrey walked up and stood there staring at the two of us. I thought Molly's jaw was going to hit the floor.

"Thanks for the offer, but no thanks." I placed my hand on his chest and swallowed hard as I felt what I'd be missing. "I'm sure you're a really sweet guy even though you want to have sex with strange women in clubs, but like I said earlier, that's not what I do. Now, if you'll excuse me, my girls are here and it's time for us to leave."

I hooked my arm in Kara's and Molly's and the four of us left the club.

"What the fuck was that?" Aubrey asked. "I would have pounded him right then and there. He was a god, Emma."

"That he was, but I don't have sex with random strangers. I know you all think it's fine and fun, but I guess I'm old fashioned."

"You're leaving tomorrow. You don't have a boyfriend. God knows when the last time you had sex was. So what do you have to lose? You can get on that plane in the morning feeling like a rock star," Molly said.

"Sorry, ladies. If you want to have sex with him, then be my guest. I'm sure he would do you all at the same time. He said you could join in." I smiled.

"You're nuts!" Kara spewed. "I never would have turned down that fine piece of ass."

Chapter 2

Before going through security at the airport, I hugged my mom goodbye.

"You be careful in New York City. I'm going to miss you, baby girl," she pouted.

"I will, Mom, and I'll miss you too. You know this is good for me. It's what I've always dreamed of."

"I know." Tears started to fill her eyes. "Now get out of here and call me when you get there so I know you arrived safely, and be careful. New York City is scary."

"I will. I love you, Mom." I laughed.

"I love you too, baby girl."

She stood there and gave me a small wave as I cleared security and headed to my gate. Just as I made my way across the airport, my flight was already boarding. With bated breath,

I stepped onto the plane, shoved my carryon in the overhead compartment, and sat in my seat, taking out my phone and checking my emails before the plane took off. My heart started racing as I opened the email from the financial department at Parsons.

Dear Miss Knight,

We are sorry to inform you that we've made a mistake in approving your financial loan for the fall semester at Parsons School of Design. We are so sorry for this inconvenience. If you still wish to attend the fall semester at Parsons, we are giving you five days to pay the tuition to hold your classes. After five days, if payment is not received in full, we will be forced to give your spot to another student.

Robert Foreman

Director of Financial Services

I couldn't even process what I was reading. How could they take my loan away at the last minute? My eyes filled with tears. My dream was no longer going to become a reality. There was no way I could afford the $21,000 fall semester tuition. I only had enough money to live off of for a while. I started to panic as my mind raced with fear. I left my mom and friends back in Florida to move to New York to attend school and now there was no school. A wave of nausea swept over me and I needed to get up and use the bathroom. As I made my way down the aisle, I noticed the bathroom was occupied. Shit. I stood there, literally shaking, waiting for whoever it was in the bathroom to get out. Suddenly, the door opened and a pair of spellbinding gray eyes looked at me.

"Hey. Emma, right?" Max smiled.

Oh my God, this can't be happening.

"Are you okay?" He lightly took hold of my arm.

"Not really. I just need to use the bathroom, please."

"Sure." He stepped out of the way.

I shut the door and stood against the sink. First Parsons and now the guy from last night? I took in a long deep breath as I tried to rationalize the situation. This wasn't the end of the world. I would go talk to the financial department tomorrow and clear everything up. When I opened the door, Max was standing there, waiting for me.

"Why are you still standing there?" I asked with irritation. He was the last person I wanted to deal with.

"I was making sure you were okay. You looked like you had tears in your eyes. Is everything okay?"

"I'm fine." I walked away and he followed behind.

I sat down in my seat and looked out the window.

"Hey, buddy, how would you like my seat in first class?" Max said to the guy sitting next to me.

"Dude, are you serious?"

"Yeah. It's seat 2A. If you don't mind, I would like to sit next to my friend here."

"Sure. I don't mind at all. Thanks." He got up from the seat and Max sat down.

"Really? You just gave up your first class seat to sit here? Are you crazy or something?"

"Maybe I am." He smiled.

Damn. His smile was just as sexy as it was last night. In fact, *he* was just as sexy as last night. Thank God I didn't sleep with him. What were the chances he would be on the same plane as me? I needed a drink and I needed one bad. The flight attendant walked by and I stopped her.

"Excuse me, can I please get a glass of red wine?"

"Sure. There's a charge for the alcoholic beverages."

"Fine."

"Drinking already?" he asked.

I looked over at him and sighed. I didn't need this shit right now. "Can you please just go back to your seat and leave me alone? I don't want to talk to anyone right now."

"Sorry, but I gave my seat up. Looks like you're stuck with me for the duration of the flight. By the way, are you traveling home?"

"No." I turned my head and looked out the window.

The flight attendant walked over and handed me my glass of wine. Before I knew it, Max reached in his pocket and pulled out some money and handed it to her.

"It's on me."

"Do you always make a habit of buying drinks for women on a plane?"

"No. Do you ever say 'thank you'?"

I sighed. "Thank you and I'm sorry. I'm just having the worst life possible right now." The sip of wine I intended to take turned into downing half the glass.

"I could tell something was wrong. Listen, I'm sorry for imposing on you. I'll just sit here and listen to some music and I won't bother you again."

Now I felt like a complete bitch. It wasn't his fault that Parsons took back my loan.

"You wanted to have sex with me last night." I smiled.

He turned his head and the corners of his mouth slightly curved. "I never said that."

"Oh, come on. You said you wanted to go somewhere and talk. That's code for 'let's go have sex.' Plus, you told me to live life on the edge and skip all the romance stuff and go straight to the bed."

He chuckled. "Okay, fine. The thought had crossed my mind. I mean, look at you, but I could tell you weren't that type of girl anyway. We had harmless flirting and you have to admit it was pretty hot."

He wasn't lying. It was hot and, unfortunately, after I left the club, I thought about him the majority of the night, which led me to take care of myself.

"You live in New York?" I asked.

"Yep. I spent the summer in Miami at our beach house, scouting out potential property for my dad's company."

"So you work for your dad?"

"Yep. I'm being groomed to take over once he retires."

"That's great." I gave a small smile.

"Since we'll probably never see each other again after this, I don't see the harm in you telling me what's wrong. Sometimes it helps to tell your problems to a complete stranger."

"You're not a stranger. I know your name and you tried to have sex with me."

He shook his head while a wide smile splayed across his gorgeous face. "All right."

I finished my wine and set the glass on the tray and Max looked away from me. He was right. I probably would never see him again after this flight, so what was the harm?

"I was moving to New York to attend Parsons School of Design. Everything was arranged. My financial loan was approved. I had been saving my money from my full-time job for living expenses and I was staying at my friend Macy's apartment while she's out of the country. Attending Parsons was a dream I had ever since I could remember. I received an email from the school this morning telling me that they made a mistake in approving my loan and that I have five days to pay the full fall tuition or else they're giving my spot to someone else."

"Wow. I'm really sorry, Emma. How can they just take it back like that?"

"I don't know. I'm going to talk to them first thing tomorrow morning." I looked out the window with tears in my eyes.

"Hey. Don't let it get you down. I bet it's just a mistake on their part."

The plane finally landed and Max took his phone off airplane mode. Several dings came through and I looked at him when he uttered, "Oh, shit."

"What's wrong?" I asked.

"Umm…nothing."

He seemed really nervous. He got up from his seat, grabbed his bag from the overhead compartment in first class, then waited for me and we walked off together.

"I have to use the bathroom."

"Okay. Well, it was great meeting you, Emma. Maybe I'll see you around New York. Good luck." He turned around and ran off.

I went into the bathroom, feeling confused and unsure of what had just happened. Oh well, I couldn't think about him. I needed to go get my bags and get to Macy's apartment and figure out what to do next. I exited the bathroom and headed towards baggage claim. Once I found it, I was startled when I heard my name.

"Emma, there you are. After I left the bathroom, I couldn't find you," Max said as he walked over and hugged me. "Go along with me. Please, Emma. I will compensate you for this favor," he whispered in my ear.

"What the fuck are you doing, Max?"

"Just smile," he said through gritted teeth.

He hooked his arm around me and walked me over to where an older woman and gentleman were standing.

"Mom, Dad, this is my fiancée, Emma." His grip around me tightened.

I gulped and looked at him with wide eyes.

"Emma, it's so nice to finally meet you," the woman said as she hugged me. "Look at you. You're beautiful."

"Emma, I'd like you to meet Bradshaw and Carol Hamilton, my parents."

"It's a pleasure to finally meet you." His dad smiled as he held out his hand.

I extended my hand and we lightly shook. "It's wonderful to meet the both of you."

Everything happened so fast I didn't know what was going on. One minute I was in the bathroom and the next, I was meeting some guy's parents who thought I was his fiancée.

"Mom, Dad. It was nice of you to come all the way here, but I have to take Emma home. We'll catch up later, okay?"

"Nonsense, son. You both will ride with us and we'll drop her off on the way."

"Seriously, Dad, we want to be alone for a while," Max commanded. "Can you please respect that?"

"Certainly we can, Max." His mom smiled. "Come on, Bradshaw. Let the two of them be for now. We can get to know Emma better at dinner tonight. Seven o'clock. Don't be late."

My eyes widened and I took in a deep breath. "Looking forward to it." I smiled.

They both walked away and exited the airport. I turned to Max, who let out a breath, and I smacked him.

"What the hell was that all about? Your fiancée? Are you fucking crazy?!"

"Ouch. Let me explain. Just calm down."

"Oh, you're going to explain. In fact, you have five seconds." I walked away when I saw my luggage come around.

I grabbed it and Max grabbed his, following me as I stepped out the doors.

Max hailed us a cab and I slid in the back seat. "Do you have the address of where you're staying?"

I pulled out the piece of paper from my purse and handed it to him.

"Tribeca, eh? Nice." He rattled off the address to the cab driver.

"Now you have three seconds to tell me what the hell just happened back there."

"Emma, it's a long story. Can it please wait until we get to your apartment?"

How could this day get any worse? I should have just stayed in Miami and none of this would be happening right now.

Chapter 3

Max slid out of the cab and held out his hand to help me. I smacked it.

"I don't need your help." I climbed out and grabbed my luggage from the cab driver. Max grabbed his and followed me inside.

"You're on floor twenty-eight," he said.

"No shit. I can read."

We took the elevator up to the twenty-eighth floor and I found apartment 28C.

"Wait. I've been here before," Max spoke. "What's your friend's name again?"

"Macy."

"Is she a high-end fashion model?"

I turned and gave him a suspicious look. "Yeah."

"I know her. I've been to a couple parties here."

"Great." I rolled my eyes as I inserted the key and opened the door. "Wow!" I exclaimed as I stepped into the foyer.

"Pretty nice. Isn't it?"

Over to the right of the foyer was the kitchen with a few white cabinets and black granite counter tops. The living room was huge with every wall being nothing but windows that overlooked the Hudson River. It was absolutely breathtaking.

"You should see the view at night with the city all lit up. It's amazing," Max said.

I turned from the window and glared at him. "Explain! NOW!" I yelled.

He put his hands up and fell back into the black leather chair.

"Okay. Okay. Can you at least sit down?"

I sat down on the couch across from the chair, waiting for him to explain himself.

"I have three months until my twenty-sixth birthday to get engaged to be married or I won't get my trust fund. It was a rule that my parents put in place when the trust fund was set up. It's what my grandparents did for my father and so now he believes because it worked for him, it'll work for me."

I waved my hands back and forth at him. "Wait a minute. In order for you to collect your trust fund, you have to be engaged by your twenty-sixth birthday? Did I just hear you right?"

"Yes, and I'll be twenty six in three months, so I would say that time is running out. I'm sorry to drag you into this, Emma, but I need your help. Trust me, I didn't plan on this. A couple of nights ago, I was drunk and apparently sent a text to my dad saying that I was bringing my fiancée home for them to meet. If you help me out with this small favor, I will help you out."

"Really? And what could you possibly do to help me out?"

"I'm going to pay for your entire tuition at Parsons. You will never have to worry about that again."

My eyes widened and my mouth dropped. "You can't be serious."

"I am. I'm in a bind, you're in a bind, and we can help each other out. All I need is for you to pretend to be my fiancée for three months. After I collect my trust fund, then you are to break the engagement off."

I couldn't believe what he was asking. He was only the guy I spoke to at a club in Miami last night and now I'm his supposed fiancée? Too much shit was spinning around in my head.

"So that's it? Are there any rules or stipulations to go with this 'arrangement'?"

"The only thing is you have to attend family and social functions. That's it. We won't be going out on dates. We won't be having sex. Unless you want to, then by all means, I'm all yours." He smiled. "Listen, Emma. In case you haven't figured it out by now, I'm not ready to settle down and, frankly, I don't have any desire to. My dad wants me to uphold the Hamilton image and create this perfect little family. Meanwhile, he's off fucking his thirty-year-old secretary and the twenty-something intern he just hired. I'm rich, successful, and soon to be even more successful and I don't need to be tied down to someone who will complicate my life."

The plan he was proposing didn't sound so bad and he was going to make my lifelong dream of attending Parsons a reality if I pretended to be his fiancée for a short period of time.

"Three months?" I asked just to be sure.

"Yes. Three months. Just until I turn twenty-six."

I placed my hands over my face and took in a deep breath. I was already here in New York. Nobody had to know about this.

It would be our little secret for three months. Three months wasn't so long.

"Okay, Max. You have yourself a deal."

He stood up in excitement. "Really, Emma? You're sure about this?"

"Yeah. I'm sure."

"Thank you so much. You have no idea how much this means to me. I'll write you a check for your tuition. Now, since we're having dinner together tonight at my parents' house, we have to go get you a ring. We have to keep it real and you can just wear it when we're together and around family."

"Now?" I asked.

"Yeah. We'll head over to Tiffany's and you can pick out whatever you want."

"Tiffany's? I've never been in Tiffany's." Excitement took over me.

"You'll love it. Let me call the family driver, Martin, to come get us."

"You have a driver?"

"Yeah. He's really cool. You're going to love this lifestyle for a while." He winked. "I think we should exchange phone numbers since we're engaged to be married." A light chuckle escaped him.

I pulled out my phone and entered in his number and he entered mine. A while later, Martin called and said he was waiting outside. My first couple of hours in New York City and I was off to pick out an engagement ring. *What the fuck am I getting myself into?*

Chapter 4

When we arrived at Tiffany's, we were taken into a room in the back where the most beautiful diamond rings sat on velvet cushions.

"It's nice to see you, Mr. Hamilton."

"Thank you, Doug. I would like to you to meet my fiancée, Emma Knight."

"It's wonderful to meet you, Miss Knight." He smiled graciously. "Please take a seat. I've taken the liberty of pulling some of our finest diamonds for you. May I offer you a glass of wine?"

My face lit up. "That would be wonderful. Thank you."

Max and I took a seat in front of the table. "Pick out whatever you want."

"They're all so beautiful, Max."

"Beautiful diamonds for a beautiful woman." He winked.

My stomach was in knots and I was afraid to touch them. I'd never seen such beauty up close before. I carefully looked at each ring as I slipped it on my left hand. Such sparkle and elegance had never touched these hands and I was in awe and feeling a bit overwhelmed.

"Here, try this one." Max smiled as he took my hand and slipped on a two-carat cushion cut ring with diamonds going down the sides.

"Excellent choice, Mr. Hamilton. That is one of our brand new collections."

"I love it." I smiled as I looked over at Max.

"Are you sure?"

"Yes, and it fits perfectly."

"That's the one we'll take, Doug." Max pulled out his credit card.

"Ah, excellent. It's so wonderful to see two young people so in love and embarking on a wonderful journey and new life together."

I almost busted out into laughter. If poor Doug only knew.

As soon as Max and I left Tiffany's, I stopped him and put my hand on his chest.

"Aren't you going to properly propose to me?" I smiled as I slipped my ring off and handed it to him.

"You mean right here on the street?"

"Yes. If we're going to be engaged, I expect a proper proposal."

"But the street is filled with people," he replied nervously.

"Isn't that the point, Max?"

He rolled his eyes and looked around. He got down on one knee and took my hand. Suddenly, people were stopped and gathered around us, watching the show.

"Emma Knight, will you marry me?"

I placed my hands over my mouth in excitement. I had to play the part of the happy girl who just got proposed to on the streets of New York.

"Yes. Oh my God, Max! Yes! I will marry you!"

He slipped the ring on my finger and stood up, pulling me into a warm embrace, one that jolted the shit out of me. His muscular arms wrapped around me were setting my body on fire.

"You'll pay for this." His hot breath trailed along my ear.

Everyone around began to clap and whistle and congratulations were said all around. Martin opened the limo door.

"Congratulations, Max and Miss Knight."

"Thank you, Martin, and please call me Emma." I smiled.

We slid into the back of the limo and Max looked at me, narrowing his eyes.

"You wanted me to do that in front of Martin. Didn't you?"

"Made it look more real. Didn't it? Now he can tell your parents how you proposed to the love of your life on the streets of New York because you're so happy and you wanted everyone to witness it."

"Damn. You're good."

"I know." I winked.

"Martin, please take us to Saks so my lovely fiancée can buy a new dress for dinner tonight."

"I have dresses, Max. I don't need to go to Saks."

"How can I put this nicely? Dinner with my parents is a formal occasion. Don't worry; I'll help you pick something out."

I guessed if I was going to play the role of a millionaire's fiancée, I'd better dress the part. Martin pulled up to the curb of Saks and opened the door for me. I climbed out and Max placed his hand on the small of my back, sending shivers down my spine. *Damn. What is it about his touch?* We took the escalator up to where the women's dresses were and, immediately, Max pulled a dress from the rack. It was a Jacquard Sheath sleeveless dress with a round neckline in natural.

"You're what? About five foot nine and a size two?"

"Size four." I smiled. "But thanks for thinking a size two."

"This will look amazing on you. Go try it on."

I took the dress from Max and the sales associate let me into the dressing room. As I took off my clothes and stood in front of the full-length mirror, I noticed some areas of toning that were desperately needed. Damn these fitting room lights. Macy said there was a fitness center in the apartment building and I could use it at any time. Tomorrow, I'd start working out. I slipped into the dress and had trouble zipping it up, so I walked out of the fitting room and asked Max, who was sitting in the chair, to help me out. He got up and walked over to me with a smile on his face as I turned around. His hand lightly took hold of the zipper and he slowly zipped it up.

"Nice light pink bra. Are you by any chance wearing matching panties?" His hot breath trailed along my neck.

I swallowed hard. "Don't you worry about what panties I'm wearing," I replied in a seductive tone.

Once again, his lips were a mere inch from my ear. "I can't help it."

I took in a deep breath and turned around. "Well?"

"That dress looks perfect on you and incredibly sexy."

"Thanks. I like it too, but I'm afraid it's too expensive."

"Nonsense. Nothing is ever too expensive for my fiancée." A smile crossed his lips.

Hell, if he wanted to buy it for me, who was I to turn down a four-hundred-dollar designer dress. I began to walk back into the fitting room when Max called my name.

"Ahem, Emma."

"Yes?" I turned around.

"Don't you need help with your zipper?"

Shit. Here we go again. My panties were already wet from when he zipped it up. I turned around and pulled my hair up. He unzipped it as slowly as he had zipped it up.

"I swear to God. If you even think about looking at my panties, I'll smack you."

"I would never. Only if you wanted me to see that sweet ass of yours, then I would."

I smirked and walked into the dressing room. As I changed back into my clothes, Max paid for the dress.

"Do you need shoes?" he asked.

"I don't know. I forgot about shoes."

"Well, let's head over to the shoe department and see what they have."

He walked a step in front of me and I couldn't help but check out his fine ass in the dark denim jeans he was wearing. He had a great body. Muscular, strong, and, from what I could tell, perfect in all areas. When we reached the shoes, a pair instantly caught my eye. I walked over to the table and picked up the thin strap, four-inch heel sandal in a natural color.

"I think these would go great with the dress." I turned the shoe over to see what size it was and my eyes diverted straight to the price. "Oh never mind." I put the shoe down.

"Why? What's wrong with them?"

"The price," I replied as I moved to another display of shoes.

"It's fine, Emma. They're only eleven hundred dollars. I've paid more than that for my own shoes. What size are you?"

"Size eight. But seriously, Max, they're too expensive."

He flagged down the sales lady and asked her if they had an eight. A few moments later, she returned with the box of shoes and I slipped my feet into them.

"They look great on you." Max smiled. "What do you think?"

"I think they're great."

"We'll take them," Max told the sales lady.

Martin was waiting for us when we stepped out of Saks. He opened the door and I slid in and across to the other side. As soon as Max slid in next to me, I lightly grabbed his hand. He looked at me with surprise and smiled.

"Thank you." A small smile fell upon my lips.

His gray eyes stared at me for a brief moment. He tilted his head as the corners of his mouth slightly curved.

"You're welcome."

I let go of his hand and looked out the window. We arrived back to my apartment and Max told me that he'd be over around six thirty to pick me up.

"I can catch a cab. You stay at your house and I'll see you when I get there."

He chuckled. "Emma, I don't live with my parents. I have my own place."

"Oh. I assumed you lived with your parents."

"Good God, no. I moved out as soon as I graduated from college. My apartment is over on East 77th Street, about twenty minutes from here, and my parents live over on Park Avenue.

"Oh, sorry about that. Then I guess I'll see you at six thirty." I grabbed the bag that my dress hung in and my shoes and went up to my new apartment.

****

I stepped into the marble tiled shower and let the hot water bead down the front of me while I tried to take in everything that happened today. I lost my loan to Parsons. I moved to New York. I got engaged to a man I just met last night, and I was going to be wearing an entire outfit that cost over fifteen hundred dollars to dinner with his parents; parents who believed that I was the love of their son's life. It was only for three months. I needed to keep reminding myself of that. I did the right thing, right? I was second guessing myself and my decision now that I was alone and had time to absorb it. I was nothing but an ordinary girl who lived in a doublewide trailer her whole life. Everything I had was worked for. Nothing was ever given to me, including the tuition payment for Parsons. I was working for that. Like an actress. Playing a role, a part; one that probably could have won me an Academy Award.

I stepped out of the shower, put on my makeup, and threw a few curls at the ends of my long, blonde hair, deciding to pull the sides back and pin it up with a pretty pearl hair clip that Aubrey bought me for my birthday. Slipping into my dress, I struggled to zip it up. Somehow, I managed and then I slipped on my ring. As I held out my hand and stared at the beauty of the diamond, there was a knock on the door.

"Hey." I gulped when I saw Max standing there in a pair of black dress pants and a white dress shirt with the top three buttons undone underneath a matching black blazer.

"You look gorgeous." He smiled as he stepped inside.

"Thanks. You're looking pretty hot yourself, Mr. Hamilton."

"Are you ready to have dinner with the folks? There's been a change of plans and we're meeting at a restaurant instead."

"As ready as I'll ever be. Let me grab my shoes."

We walked out of the apartment building and climbed into the back seat of a Rolls Royce.

"Emma, I would like you to meet Darren. He's another one of my drivers."

"Hi, Darren. Nice to meet you."

"Nice to meet you too, Emma." He smiled as he looked back at me.

"Darren is the only one who knows about our little arrangement. I trust him with my life. If you need him for anything, you are to give him a call. He'll take you wherever you need to go. Hand me your phone and I'll put his number in for you."

"I thought no one was supposed to know."

He put in Darren's number and handed me my phone as he placed his fingers under my chin.

"Like I said, I trust him with my life."

Chapter 5

We stepped inside Shay Gardens and I was blown away by the décor. Round tables spread across the two-level restaurant with gold-colored tablecloths and beautifully lit candles that sat in the center. The dark wood trim that surrounded the restaurant was elegantly carved and the finest paintings hung on the walls. The hostess showed us to the table where Max's parents were waiting for us.

"You've arrived." His mom smiled as she lightly hugged Max and then me. "You look stunning, Emma."

"Thank you." I smiled as Max pulled out my chair.

I looked over and saw a beautiful young girl sitting across from me. "Emma, I would like you to meet Fiona, my sister."

"Hello, Fiona."

"Hey," she said with a fake smile. I could tell already that she didn't like me.

"Oh my God!" Max's mom exclaimed as she grabbed my left hand. "You got your ring. It's beautiful."

"Yes, it is. You did a nice job, Max." His dad smiled.

"Have you two set the date yet?" Fiona glared at Max.

"No. Not yet. It probably won't be for a couple of years. Emma wants to finish school first."

Both his parents grilled me about my background and my childhood. I had to make it sound better than it was because they'd think I wasn't good enough for their son. Hell, I didn't think I was good enough for him. I told them I grew up in Miami in a very influential neighborhood and that both my parents were very successful business people. I didn't want to give out too much information in case they decided to check out my story. I wouldn't put it past these people, especially ones that would put an engagement stipulation on their son's trust fund. After we finished dinner and dessert, we said our goodbyes and climbed into the Rolls Royce.

"What a success! My parents adore the shit out of you."

"I'm not so sure about your sister."

"Ignore her. She's seventeen going on thirty. She has an opinion about everything and everyone."

Max reached in his pocket and handed me a check. "This is for your first year at Parsons. Go deposit it in the bank tomorrow and then pay your tuition. I don't want you losing out on your classes."

Suddenly, guilt washed over me and I found it hard to accept it.

"What's wrong?"

"Nothing. Thanks, Max. I really appreciate it."

He placed his hand on mine and gave it a gentle squeeze. My heart skipped a beat at his touch.

"No, Emma, thank you. I wouldn't be able to pull this off without you."

I gave him a small smile as the Rolls Royce pulled up to my building. "I'll talk to you tomorrow. Good night, Max," I said before climbing out and shutting the door.

"Good night, Emma."

****

I slept in longer than I should have, but I was exhausted from all the shit that had happened yesterday. When I awoke, I looked at the ring on my finger that I forgot to take off before climbing into bed. Today was a new day and I was still engaged. Somehow, as I slept, I prayed to the dream gods to let it all be a really bad dream; a dream that happened while I was still sleeping in Miami. But it wasn't a dream. I let out a long stretch before climbing out of bed. I shuffled into the kitchen for a cup of coffee and noticed there wasn't a coffeemaker. *What the fuck? Who doesn't own a coffee maker?* No time for a shower. I needed coffee ASAP. I dug out a pair of black yoga pants, an oversized pink t-shirt that said, "I'm All Yours," and threw on my pink Miami baseball cap. After grabbing my purse and phone, I took the elevator down to the lobby and headed out the door. Right or left? Shit. I didn't know New York City yet. I walked back inside and asked Tommy, the doorman, where the closest Starbucks was.

"Go out the door, make a right, and it's right on the corner."

"Thanks, Tommy." I smiled at him.

"You're welcome, Emma."

I found Starbucks and stood in a line with about fifteen other people who had the same idea I had. Finally, it was my turn. I ordered a coffee and a banana chip muffin and took a seat at a table by the window. My phone started beeping with a text message from Kara.

"How's New York City? I figured I would have heard from you by now."

"Sorry. Yesterday was kind of a crazy day trying to get situated."

"Meet any hot guys yet?"

"Not yet."

I couldn't tell her about Max. As much as I wanted to, I couldn't. The questions would start being asked and I would have to lie to my best friends. It was better that they knew nothing of what happened yesterday.

"Keep me posted and send me lots of snap chats. Especially when a hot guy is around."

"Tell the girls I said hi and I promise to keep in touch."

As I sipped my coffee, I wondered what Max was doing. I caught myself thinking about him a lot already today. In some sort of weird way, I missed his company. Hell, he was practically the only person I knew in New York City, so that would explain why I missed him, not to mention the fact that all I could think about was what he looked like naked. I finished my coffee and muffin and hailed a cab to the bank to open a new account and then to Parsons School of Design. When I stepped into the large building, I asked the guy sitting behind the desk where the financial office was. He guided me down the hall, to the right, and then another right.

"What may I do for you?" the old woman with a unibrow asked.

"I'm here to pay for my fall semester."

It didn't matter anymore, why the hell they decided to decline my loan at the last minute, so I didn't even bother asking. I handed the lady my I.D. and then handed her a money order for the tuition.

"You're all set. I hope you enjoy your time here at Parsons." She smiled.

I wanted to tell her thanks for nothing, but I just gave her a small smile and left. Classes started in a few days and I was more than ready. Before heading back to the apartment, I decided to stop at the store and pick up a few things, the most important item being a coffeemaker and coffee. I purchased some snacks and some food to cook meals since Macy's refrigerator and cabinets were empty. I wasn't surprised with her being a model and all. She always ate like a rabbit. My hands were full of bags, the coffeemaker being the heaviest. I tried to hail a cab, but they weren't stopping. I set down my bags and pulled out my phone, pulling up Darren's number.

"Hello, Miss Knight. Do you need me to pick you up?"

"Hi, Darren. Yes, please. I'm outside of Whole Foods by Parsons. I'm not sure exactly what street I'm on."

"No worries. I'll find you. I'm in the general area right now. Sit tight and I'll be there shortly."

"Thank you." *Click.*

I stood there with my heavy bags and watched the people pass by as I felt like I was in another world. A few moments passed and the Rolls Royce pulled up. Darren got out, opened the door, and took my bags.

"Thank you, Darren. I didn't want to call you, but I couldn't get a cab to stop and these bags are heavy."

"No problem, Emma. I'm at your disposal whenever you need me."

I slid in the back and then asked Darren if he'd seen Max today.

"Yes, I just dropped him and a lady friend of his off at a restaurant for an early dinner."

Something happened to me. My stomach instantly felt sick. "Oh, good for him. I'm going to go home and cook a nice meal for myself."

He looked at me from the rearview mirror and smiled. Darren was a nice man. He was about mid to late forties with brown hair and hazel-colored eyes. There was something about him that clicked with me and I felt comfortable around him. Almost like a father figure. We reached my building and Darren helped me carry my bags up to my apartment.

"Thank you. I appreciate your help." I smiled.

"You're welcome, Emma. Have a good night." He walked toward the door, stopped, and turned to me. "Are you sure you know what you're doing with Max?"

I was taken aback by his question. "Yeah, I know what I'm doing."

He pursed his lips. "You're a great girl and I don't want to see you get hurt. Sometimes, people need to fall on their own before they'll learn a valuable life lesson." He walked out the door, shutting it behind him.

I stood there for a moment and pondered what he meant. I figured he was talking about Max. After setting up my new coffeemaker and putting my food away, I decided to cook myself a breaded chicken breast and a baked potato. As I was preparing dinner, I had the music playing on my phone and "Uptown Funk" came on. I needed to distract my mind from Max. I began dancing around the small kitchen and using a wooden spoon as a microphone, moving my hips back and forth while I breaded the chicken. I threw it in the oven with the baked potato and shut the door while moving to the beat of the music and singing. I turned around and screamed when I saw Max standing there, smiling at me.

"What the FUCK! You scared the shit out of me, Max!" I turned off the music.

"Sorry, but I knocked. You didn't hear me and you didn't lock the door, so I let myself in and watched your sexy dance moves. Damn, Emma. Rule number one when living in New York: always lock your door."

"I forgot. I thought you were on a date."

"How did you know that?" he asked as he arched his eyebrow.

"Darren told me. I had to have him pick me up from Whole Foods because I had a lot of bags and I couldn't catch a cab. I was surprised I didn't hear from you today."

"I was busy at work. Pretty much in meetings all day."

A smart-ass remark was about to escape my lips, but I stopped it.

"I take it you're cooking dinner."

"Yep. I haven't eaten since this morning. So, what are you doing here? And why is your date over already?"

"I only took her to dinner. Once we left the restaurant, I took her home and headed here."

"Why?" I asked as I poured a glass of wine. "Would you like some?"

"Sure. Thanks. And why what?" He took a seat on the stool in front of the counter.

"Why would you cut your date short to come here? You didn't want to have sex with her?"

"Of course I did, but she's on her period and I don't do that shit. I don't think you should be asking me questions like that."

I handed him his glass. "Why not? We are engaged to be married after all."

A twinge of pain invaded my heart when he admitted he wanted to have sex with her. What the hell was going on with me? It had been too long since I'd had sex. The last time was with Justin and that was right before we broke up six months ago. Speak of the devil. My phone rang and his name popped up.

"Ah, shit." I looked at Max and then answered the call.

"Hello."

"Emma, it's Justin."

"I know who it is, Justin. Why are you calling?"

I looked at Max and he stared back with narrowed eyes.

"I heard you moved to New York to go to that design school or whatever. Why did you do that?"

"Gee, Justin, maybe because it has always been a lifelong dream of mine. You would know that if you ever paid attention to me in our relationship." I put it on speaker and set the phone down. I had to check on the chicken.

"I paid attention to you and, by the way, you never paid me for that X-box game you purposely broke."

Before the laugher could escape him, Max covered his mouth.

"I'll send a check in the mail."

"I miss you, Emma. I really do," he spoke in a sad tone.

"Sorry about that, Justin. Listen, I need to go. My dinner is ready. Do me a favor and please don't call me anymore."

"Is that what you truly want?" he asked.

"Yes. I'm living life in New York now. I'm starting over. I suggest you do the same."

"Goodbye, Emma." *Click.*

A single tear rose up in my eye, and Max got up from his stool and walked over to me.

"Hey, you okay?" he asked softly.

"Yeah. He's an idiot and he has a lot of growing up to do."

"Go sit down and I'll put your food on the plate and bring it to you."

"I'm fine, Max. I can—"

He placed his hand on my shoulder. "Emma, go sit down. Please."

I took my glass of wine and the bottle and sat down at the table. Max put the chicken on a plate and fixed my baked potato with a little bit of butter, salt, and pepper. He set it down in front of me with a knife and a fork and took the seat across from me.

"Would you like a bite?" I cut into the chicken.

"Nah. I'm full. How long have you and Justin been broken up?"

"Six months."

"How long did you date?"

"A little over a year."

"Wow. So, you broke his X-box game?" He smirked.

I took a bite of my potato and nodded my head. "He wouldn't listen to me. That was the biggest problem in our relationship. I would talk and he'd zone out. He was either watching sports or playing his damn X-box. He didn't have a job and he never took me out. Even when I offered to pay, he still wouldn't go."

"He sounds like a loser."

"He is. I got so fed up that I couldn't take it anymore. I went over to his apartment and he was playing X-box. I asked him to turn it off because I needed to talk to him. He told me that it was cool and just to start talking. So I did and he basically ignored me. I told him we were over and he told me not to be silly. He never looked at me once the whole time I was talking to him. Rage got the best of me so I took the disc out of the X-box and stomped on it until it broke into several pieces."

Max chuckled. "What did he do?"

"He cried."

He threw his head back in laughter. "Jesus Christ, Emma."

I couldn't help but laugh with him. He held up his wine glass.

"Here's to broken X-box games and the start of a new life."

I held up my glass and we lightly clanked them together. After finishing my dinner, Max got up from his seat.

"I better get going. I have to be at the office early tomorrow." I got up and walked him to the door.

"Thanks for stopping by."

"You're welcome. Thanks for the wine." His eyes stared straight at me. He hesitated for a moment and then walked out the door. "Good night, Emma."

"Good night, Max."

I shut the door, locked it, and then leaned up against it. There was a part of me that didn't want him to leave.

Chapter 6

I spent the next couple of days inside my apartment building. I got up in the mornings, went down to the fitness center, worked out, and then sat in front of the TV all day. The only person I knew in New York was Max and I hadn't heard from him since the night he was over. He was probably too busy trying to fuck anything with legs. School started tomorrow and I couldn't wait. I needed to keep myself busy and immerse myself in something other than thinking about him all day. What I thought was going to be easy wasn't turning out that way. He had an effect on me that I couldn't explain and all I wanted to do was spend time with him. Maybe it was just because I was in a strange city and living alone that I felt this way. I needed to get out and meet more people. I talked to my mom back in Miami and she was doing well. I'd never kept anything from her before and it was hard not to tell her about Max. I missed my girls – Kara, Aubrey, and Molly – and I missed going out. After putting on my pajamas and climbing into bed, my phone beeped with a text message from Max.

"Good luck on your first day of school tomorrow."

Really? I don't hear from him in two days and he sends me that? I put my phone down and didn't respond. Turning off my light, I snuggled under the covers and closed my eyes.

****

I arrived and took a seat in my Integrative Studio 1 class. I was nervous as hell just like any other person would be when they start something new and unfamiliar.

"Hi, I'm Hannah." The girl next to me sat down and smiled.

"Hi, I'm Emma." A prospective friend already. I was excited.

We sat and talked for a few minutes before our, oh my God, sexy as shit professor walked in. He scanned the class and smiled, welcoming us. I swear I felt my ovaries explode when he looked at me. He stood a little over six feet tall with messy brown hair and a light beard that sat upon his perfectly sculpted jawline. I frowned when my gaydar started flying off the charts. When class let out, Hannah and I found that we had the next two classes together. Before our last class, we took a lunch break and grabbed sandwiches at Breads Bakery. She was a cute girl with curly brown hair and big brown eyes. Her tiny body fitted her five-foot-four stature. She was from Iowa and was in New York cultural shock. She lived in one of the campus apartments and was shocked when I told her where I lived. I explained to her that it was Macy's place and she was letting me stay there. As we were talking and getting to know each other, my phone beeped with a message from Max.

"You didn't respond to my text last night. I expect a response when I send you a message."

"At lunch now. Can't talk. TTYL!"

I smiled, and before I set my phone down, another message came through.

"I'm coming over tonight."

"Hey, would you mind if I sat with you lovely ladies?" a handsome guy asked. "I'm Austin. I was sitting behind you two in the last two classes."

"Hi, Austin." I smiled. "I'm Emma and this is Hannah."

Another potential friend. This day was turning out better than I thought it would. Austin was the same age as Hannah and me. He lived with his boyfriend, who was six years older than he was, in a studio apartment in SoHo. The two of them moved to New York from California over the summer when his boyfriend took a job on Wall Street. After finishing our lunch, we walked back to Parsons and headed to our last class of the day. When I walked out of the building, I noticed Darren standing in front of the Rolls Royce.

"Good day, Emma. I'm here to drive you home."

"Hi, Darren. He's not in there, is he?"

He chuckled. "No. You're safe."

I smiled as he opened the door and I slid into the back seat.

"How was your first day of school?"

"It was good. I met some new friends."

He looked at me through his rearview mirror. "That's great, Emma. I'm glad you had a good day."

I opened the door to my apartment and stepped inside, setting my bag on the floor. The last text message Max sent me was that he was coming over tonight, but he didn't say if we were going to dinner or not. So I decided to ask him.

"What time are you coming over? Are we doing dinner?"

"I won't be over until after nine and I already have dinner plans."

FUCKER. He pissed me off again.

"Why are you coming over? I've had a long day and I'm tired."

"I have to talk to you about the engagement party my parents are throwing us and I won't stay long."

Really? An engagement party? Shit. I pulled out some menus that I had found in the kitchen drawer and decided to place a delivery order from the Chinese restaurant around the block. I changed into a pair of sweatpants and a tank top and put my hair up in a high ponytail. A while later, my dinner had arrived and I took it over to the couch with a glass of wine and turned on the episode of *Revenge* I was on during my two-day *Revenge* marathon. It was eight forty-five when I heard a knock. I set my carton of sweet and sour chicken down and walked to the door, looking out the peephole to make sure it was Max. I opened the door and, instantly, his eyes traveled from my head down to my feet. I almost lost my breath when I saw him standing there in his dark gray business suit.

"How was school?" he asked as he walked in.

"It was good."

"You're eating Chinese, I see."

I sighed and took a seat on the couch, picking up my carton and a piece of chicken with my chopsticks. He sat down next to me.

"My parents are throwing us an engagement party next weekend at their home."

"And? You couldn't have told me that over the phone?"

"I hadn't seen you in a couple of days." His fingers played with the ends of my ponytail. "I wanted to tell you in person."

I turned my head towards him so my hair was out of his reach. "How was your dinner?"

"Boring. It was with a prospective client. Why don't you tell me about your day?" He softly smiled.

"Well, let's see. I went to class, met some new friends, had lunch, and now I'm home. That pretty much sums it up."

"What's wrong with you? I'm sensing an attitude." His fingers deftly ran across my shoulder.

I shuddered.

"Nothing's wrong and I don't have an attitude." I did have an attitude, but I didn't want to. The fact that he walked into my life unexpectedly and decided to turn my world upside down irritated me. The more I was with him, and the more I stared into his amazing gray eyes, the harder I was falling.

"Tell me about your new friends."

I got up from the couch and took my Chinese cartons into the kitchen. "Their names are Hannah and Austin and they're really nice."

"Austin?"

I swore I heard a hint of jealousy in his voice and there was no way I was telling him that he was gay.

"Yeah. He lives in a studio apartment over in SoHo and Hannah lives on campus."

"I'm glad you met some people. So I suppose you'll be going out with them some time?"

I narrowed my eyes at his question.

"Yeah. I'm sure I will be."

He got up and walked to the door. "I better get going."

I stood in front of him as he stared at me for a few moments before placing his thumb on my chin.

"You look really hot in that outfit."

My toes curled and my heart picked up a rapid pace.

"Are you trying to have sex with me again?"

He kissed my forehead. "No. I just wanted to tell you that." He smiled and walked out the door.

****

I knew what I was getting myself into by agreeing to this arrangement. I knew that when I saw him for the first time in

Miami and my body started to tingle that I was interested in him, but I didn't think I'd ever see him again. The more days that went by and I didn't see or talk to Max, the more dejected I became. I barely knew him but yet we were engaged and he was paying for my school. It was a Saturday morning and I had just gotten out of bed when my phone beeped with a text message from Darren.

"Good morning, Emma. Max is sending me over to pick you up and bring you to his apartment. I should be there in about fifteen minutes."

I sighed.

"I just woke up and I need to shower and get dressed. You can tell Mr. Hamilton that I'll be over when I'm done getting ready and no sooner. So I'll see you in about an hour."

Who the hell did Max think he was? I thought I had heard my phone beep as I was showering, so when I finished, I took it from the nightstand in my room.

"Don't eat breakfast. I have breakfast here for us."

I rolled my eyes. What the hell was he doing?

I stepped out of the building and Darren was waiting at the curb.

"Good morning, Emma." He smiled.

"To what do I owe the pleasure of being summoned so early in the morning by Mr. Hamilton?"

Darren snickered. "I'm not quite sure."

He drove me to Max's apartment and pulled around to the parking garage where an elevator sat at the far end.

"Take that elevator up to the top floor."

"Thanks, Darren. Have a good day."

"You too, Emma."

Chapter 7

I grabbed my purse, climbed out of the Rolls Royce, and took the elevator up to the thirtieth floor. As the doors opened, I stepped into the foyer of Max's apartment. I nearly had an orgasm when I saw him walking towards me in a pair of faded blue jeans and no shirt. I gulped at the sight of his ripped abs and the hint of his V that peeked out from where his jeans sat low on his hips. Actually, I think I did have an orgasm.

"Good morning, Emma. Welcome to my apartment."

"Good morning, Max."

I needed to keep my cool because it was taking every bit of strength I had not to tackle him to the ground and rape him. This wasn't like me and I blamed it on not having sex for so long. I was only human, after all.

"Come sit down and join me for breakfast."

I followed him to the kitchen where the smell of eggs and bacon infiltrated the place. His kitchen was huge with top-of-the-line appliances, dark cherry cabinets, and black speckled granite counter tops. I took a seat at the modern black elongated table and Max handed me a cup of coffee.

"Thanks. Are you going to tell me why you sent your driver to pick me up? And, by the way, what happened to Martin?"

He chuckled. "Martin is the family's driver and Darren is my personal driver. No one uses him but me. I use Martin when I'm in a pinch. Anyway, I wanted to have breakfast with you."

"Why?" I asked. "I hadn't heard from or seen you but once this week."

"Exactly, and I felt it was time we saw each other." He set a plate of eggs and bacon down in front of me.

"So YOU felt it was time to see each other? What if I didn't feel that way?"

"You're here, aren't you?" He smirked.

Damn him. "You're lucky I didn't have any plans today."

"I guess I am." He sat down across from me with a smile. "Have you told any of your friends back home about us?"

"No. Why would I? After our deal is over, we won't be seeing each other anymore. Why try to explain that to them?"

"I guess. Don't forget the engagement party is next Saturday night and my mom is already asking why I haven't brought you by the house. I told her you had just started classes and you've been really busy but that we'll come by tomorrow for dinner."

"What? I have plans tomorrow."

"Cancel them," he commanded.

I didn't really have plans yet, but I wanted him to think I did. I couldn't help but to stare at his rock hard chest as I consumed my breakfast.

"You really need to put on a shirt."

"Why? Are you getting excited looking at me?"

"You're very bold, Max, and no, I'm not. I just don't think that you should sit at the table with no shirt on."

"Why don't you take yours off and then maybe you wouldn't feel so uncomfortable." The corners of his mouth curved upwards.

My panties were getting wet by the second and I was horny as hell. All my dignity went out the window. I guess that's what lack of sex does to you.

"Fine." I lifted my shirt over my head and tossed it on the floor.

He gasped and slowly shook his head. My heart was racing as he got up from his chair and walked over to me, holding out his hand.

I took it and he helped me up.

"Are you trying to get me to fuck you?" he slyly asked.

"I guess I am. It's been a long time since I've had sex and I'm horny as hell. We are engaged to be married, after all," I nervously spoke.

"Indeed we are."

He ran his fingers along my collarbone and down the center of my breasts. I took in a deep breath as he stared into my eyes.

"You're so beautiful, Emma, and I want to fuck you so badly. But I need to make sure that this is what you want." His lips suddenly became dangerously close to mine. I knew once they touched, there was no turning back.

"It is what I want," I whispered. "But wait."

"What is it?" he asked with concern.

"Shit. I'm on the pill and you can't use a condom. I'm allergic to the latex unless you have non-latex ones."

"Seriously? You're allergic to condoms?" His smile grew wide.

"Yes. I'm serious. It's a disaster down there if latex touches it."

"If you're trying to ask me if I have an STD, you don't have to worry about that. I always use a condom. ALWAYS. Except this time." I could see the excitement dancing around in his eyes.

I glared at him. "You always use a condom?"

"Yes, Emma. I swear to you I'm clean."

"Okay, then."

He placed his hand around the nape of my neck and his lips touched mine, softly at first and testing the waters. His earthy and warm scent that radiated off him sent my pheromones into high gear. My lips parted by force of his tongue and I responded by introducing mine to his. My body was on fire and I was raring to go. He cupped his hands around my ass, squeezing tight as I jumped up and wrapped my legs around him so he could carry me to wherever it was he wanted to fuck me. A subtle moan escaped him as he carried to me to the couch, turning around and sitting down so I was straddling him. His erection pressed against me and it felt so good. I softly moaned as his tongue traveled from my mouth and down to my neck.

"You have me so fucking hard, Emma." His hands unclasped my bra and he took the straps down, throwing it across it room.

He pushed me back so he could have a look at my bare breasts. Pulling my body closer, he took my hard nipple between his lips and moaned as he gently sucked on it. Excitement had moved through me and, oh my God, I was coming. I couldn't stop it and I was embarrassed because that had never happened to me before. He stopped and looked at me.

"Did you just come?"

I nodded.

"Fuck, baby. That is so hot. We have to slow down for a minute," he said with bated breath.

He lifted me off of him and took my hand, leading me to the other side of the apartment where his bedroom was. We stopped in front of his king-sized bed and he slowly unbuttoned my pants and slid them off my hips.

"Look at you. Your body is what every man dreams of." His hands softly ran down my body and to the inside of my thighs. He gazed at me as his fingers moved to the crotch of my panties. His eyes slowly closed and he took in a sharp breath. "You are so wet. We better get these off of you." I took them down before his finger dipped inside and worked its way around me, exploring and hitting the right spots.

I moaned as I unbuttoned his jeans and grasped the sides, taking them down and releasing his throbbing rock hard cock.

"No underwear?" I smiled.

"I forgot to put some on this morning." Another finger plunged inside me and I gasped, losing air as excitement enveloped me.

My hand wrapped around his manhood, taking in his amazing pleasurable orgasmic length and thickness. A soft moan escaped his lips as his hot breath trailed along my neck.

"My mouth is greedy for your pussy, Emma, and I need to taste you." Removing his fingers from me, he gently laid me down on the bed and hovered over me for a moment, brushing strands of my hair from my forehead. His mouth gently met mine before trailing down to my breasts and taking each hardened peak into his mouth before his tongue slowly slid down my torso, stopping at my belly button and tracing tiny circles around it. My stomach tightened and my pussy began to quiver. His head made its way between my legs as his tongue slid up my inner thigh, teasing me and taking hold of every sexual sensation ever felt.

"Do you want my mouth on your pussy, Emma?" he whispered between my legs with the feel of his hot breath inches from me.

"Yes, Max. Now. Please," I begged as my fingers tangled in his hair. And there it was. His tongue slid up my wet opening as he groaned and flickered at my clit, causing an orgasmic sensation to build. He circled around my opening before spreading my legs farther apart as his mouth devoured me. I threw my head back in excitement as I arched my back and lifted my hips, begging for him to go deeper.

"Ah, baby. I can't wait to thrust my dick inside you," he spoke as the sensation built and my body tensed, releasing myself to him.

He lifted his head and ran his tongue across his lips as his mouth smashed into mine, and before I knew it, he pushed himself inside of me, immersing me with his cock. We both gasped.

"You're so tight. Shit, Emma. Your pussy is so fucking hot inside."

He pounded into me as I wrapped my legs tightly around his waist. His hands reached down and grasped my ass, slightly lifting me up so he could penetrate me deeper. Our moans grew louder with each thrust as his balls smacked against my bare skin. My heart was pounding out of my chest and my skin was overheated. My God, this had to be the best sex I'd ever had. My body was building and my release was close.

"Are you about to come, Emma?" he asked with bated breath.

"Yes," I exclaimed.

I could feel his body tense as he threw his head back, thrusting into me deep and hard, throwing me into the throes of yet another amazing orgasm. His last thrust halted as he stared into my eyes and spilled himself deep inside me. He collapsed on top of me and lay there as our heart rates slowed and our breathing returned to normal. He sat up and kissed my lips before rolling off of me.

"That was amazing." He smiled.

"It sure was. Thank you." I got up from the bed. I needed to play it off as that was all I wanted. No cuddling, no talking, nothing. If I cuddled, I'd fall. If I fell, I'd break. I just needed sex. That was all.

"Where do you think you're going?"

"I'm getting dressed." I smiled.

"Why? Get back in bed."

I turned around and looked at him, narrowing my eyes. "Max, we fucked. That's it." I put on my clothes and went back to the kitchen and poured a cup of coffee.

"Really, Emma?"

I turned around. "What?"

"You're just going to up and leave like that?"

I silently laughed because wasn't that what he did? "We both knew it was inevitable, Max. We were going to have sex sooner or later. But that's all it is. In three months, we'll never have to see each other again."

Saying that hurt me in places I never knew could hurt. I needed to keep my head in the game because this was what it was. It was a deal. A three-month arrangement and then it would be over. It would be easy for him to walk away because he'd get his trust fund, the only thing he cared about. For me, it wouldn't be so easy if I became emotionally involved.

"I guess you're right. But still."

"Isn't that why you brought me here? I mean, come on. You were practically naked when I got here. Admit it; you brought me here hoping we'd have sex."

He looked at me and narrowed his eyes. "Sorry, Emma, but that's not why I brought you here. The reason I brought you here is because I thought we could spend the day together at Central Park. Since you've been in New York, you haven't been there yet. At least, I don't think you have."

"No. I haven't."

He stepped closer to me and smiled as he placed his thumb on my chin. "Would you like to go to Central Park with me?"

"Sure." I gave a small smile.

Chapter 8

Central Park was nothing like I'd ever seen in my life. It had to be the most beautiful place on Earth. At least to me it was. This wasn't an ordinary park; it was another world. The only park I ever went to growing up was the one by my house in Miami. A small piece of land with a few swings and overgrown grass that wasn't regularly cut. We were near mid-park when I spotted a familiar statue ahead.

"Is that what I think it is?" I asked in excitement.

"Depends on what you think it is." Max smiled.

As I approached the sculpture, I was in awe of the beauty standing before me.

"Oh my God, it is. It's Alice in Wonderland. That was one of my favorite Disney movies when I was a child."

I climbed up and ran my hand along the bronzed mushroom that Alice was sitting on.

"Sit down and I'll take your picture." Max smiled.

Suddenly, I felt like a kid again as I became giddy and sat in front of Alice while Max snapped a picture.

"Come up here and we'll take a selfie." I waved my hand for him to join me.

He climbed up the statue and sat down next to me. He held up his phone in front of us and snapped a picture.

"I have an idea," he spoke as he took my hand and helped me down. We walked over to where the horse and carriages were parked. Max pulled out a wad of cash, handed it to the man in the carriage, and then helped me up. "Have you ever been on a carriage ride?" he asked.

"No." I smiled as I sat down.

"Well, now you can say you have. We're going to tour Central Park in style, Miss Knight."

As we sat in the carriage, I took in the beauty of Central Park. I felt like a princess for the first time in my life and, I must say, I enjoyed it.

"Why don't you tell me about your real childhood," Max spoke as he looked at me.

"There's not that much to tell. My dad left us when I was two and my mom struggled her whole life to support us. She got pregnant with me at seventeen and dropped out of school. My grandparents were upset and kicked her out. When I was old enough to work, I got a job, finished school, and then worked full-time to help her with the bills. My childhood was not a magical one but my mom did the best she could and she worked really hard. I couldn't fault her for that."

"She never married?"

"No. She dated a few guys for a while, but they always turned out to be lazy jerks. Kind of like Justin. It took me a while, but I finally saw the kind of person he was and where his life was going, which was nowhere, and I wasn't going to be stuck with someone like that. I have goals and dreams for myself."

"You certainly do, Emma." He smiled.

"What about your childhood? It couldn't have been all bad growing up rich and spoiled."

He chuckled. "It wasn't all that grand. I was more of a trophy for my mom and dad than anything. Their first born, and a son at that, who would take over my father's company and carry on the Hamilton name and image. Everything in my life, since the day I was born, was carefully planned and calculated. The private school I went to, the friends I was allowed to hang out with, even the college I attended."

"Which was?"

"Columbia. I had to follow in my father's footsteps and even join the same fraternity he was in. It was like he was reliving his youth through me and I hated it."

"What about your sister?"

"She's going through the same thing, but she's more of a rebel than I was. They are the reason why I won't settle down with anyone. It's all a show."

"Does your mom know about your dad's affairs?"

"I don't think so and, if she does, she's stupid not to have left him by now. But she's just as money hungry as he is, so I'm not sure she'd ever give up the Hamilton name or lifestyle. One time, we were on vacation in Hawaii and my mom had taken ill with a migraine. My dad took me and my sister down to the beach and then told us to stay and build sand castles while he went and talked to someone he knew. I watched him as he walked up the beach and to a hotel room not too far from where me and Fiona were playing. After a while, I got up and peeked inside the door wall that I saw him go through and watched him fucking some other woman. I'll never forget the feeling of sickness and disappointment that shot through me."

"I'm sorry, Max. How old were you?"

"Thirteen. It was at that moment that I realized what a fake he was."

"Did he know you saw him?"

"No. But it was that day that I started acting differently towards him. He wasn't my hero anymore. A few years later, I was at a hotel, having lunch with one of my friends who was staying there, and I saw my dad and some woman walk through the lobby and to the elevator. I quickly got up from my seat and watched them get on the elevator and go up to the third floor. I ran up the stairwell and made it just in time as they got off the elevator and watched what room they went to. I sat up against the wall outside the room and listened to the moans that came from inside. It made me sick. For some reason, I thought that maybe Hawaii was a one-time thing with him. When the moans stopped, I knocked on the door. I wanted nothing more than that asshole to get caught. Surprisingly enough, he opened it with a towel wrapped around his waist. The look on his face was priceless. I just shook my head at him and left. Later that night, he took me out and said he was sorry and that he'd never do it again. He told me that if I told my mom, I'd be cut off and lose everything. There was no use in hurting my mom anyway."

There was a sadness in his voice when he spoke about his childhood. Here was a man who had the world at his fingertips but was unhappy. I grabbed his hand and he looked over at me with a small smile.

"I'm sorry he's such an ass. But I don't think you're anything like him if that's what you're worried about."

"Not really. I just don't have any desire to be tied down to one woman for the rest of my life and play the happy little married couple with the perfect family. It's not my style. I don't like to answer to anyone. I do what I do and I do what I please. I don't need some girl trying to control me. I watch my mom try and do it with my dad and look what's going on in that relationship."

I didn't know what to say at that moment. I was in shock that he would even say something like that to me. "Hang in there, Hamilton." I smiled.

"I am." He kissed the side of my head.

****

We grabbed some lunch at the Central Park boathouse and, as I was sipping my wine, Max looked at me in a panic.

"Take the ring off. Now!"

What the hell? I slid the ring off and clenched it tightly in my hand just as a beautiful, tall, dark-haired woman approached us.

"Hey, Max," she said as she looked at him and then over at me, giving me the bitch look.

"Hey, Aria."

"We still on for tonight? Remember you said you'd take me to that new club that just opened up?"

"A new club opened? How did I not know about this? I would love to go with the two of you." I smiled.

First, his eyes widened before he narrowed them at me.

"I'm sorry, but who is she?" Aria asked.

"So rude of me not to introduce myself. I'm Emma. It's nice to meet you. I'm a friend of Max."

I held out my hand and she looked down at it and turned away. Ah, this was going to be fun.

"Emma, I don't think that club is really your scene," Max spoke.

"Really? I happen to love clubs. So it's settled. Aria and I would love for you to take us."

"Then I'm not going!" Aria chimed like a two-year-old on the verge of a tantrum.

"Oh, please, Aria. Do come. I'm kind of thinking right now that since it's a new club and all, that it would be packed with people and you'd have to wait in an incredibly long line with the hopes that they let you in. Max, on the other hand, can pull some strings and get us right in. Am I right?" I smiled at Max.

"Yeah," he said, deadpan.

"Fine. Pick me up at eight o'clock." She stomped away from the table and I couldn't help but laugh.

"What the fuck do you think you're doing?" Max asked in seriousness.

"Please. Get over yourself. I just need a ride. I won't be hanging with you two lovebirds. I'll call Hannah and Austin and ask them to meet me there."

He shook his head at me. "This isn't a game, Emma."

"I never said it was, Max." I took a sip of my wine and slipped my ring back on.

Chapter 9

Hannah, Austin, and his boyfriend, Dominic, were going to meet me at the club. I honestly didn't know what possessed me to say that I'd go. It was probably the sick feeling I got when Aria said that Max would take her. My body was still on fire from the morning sex we'd had and I couldn't get it out of my head. I looked at myself in the black sheer, spaghetti-strap, baby-doll dress with the jewel-accented empire waist and smiled. I bought it back in Miami for a friend's wedding but didn't get the chance to wear it since she called the wedding off. I slipped into a pair of black, round toe, stiletto heels with a bow and sprayed my curly up-do one last time before the doorbell rang. When I opened the door, Darren was standing there, smiling at me.

"Good evening, Emma. Are you ready?"

"Hi, Darren. Just let me grab my clutch." I hooked my arm in his as we walked down the hallway. "Is she in the car?" I asked.

He looked at me with a sly grin. "Yes. She's in there. Are you sure you know what you're doing?"

"Not really." I smiled.

He opened the door and I slid inside next to Max. I swear he gasped when he saw me.

"Hello, Emma," he spoke.

"Hi, Max. Hey, Aria. You look really pretty." *As pretty as a hooker waiting on the street corner.*

"Hey." The only word she could seem to muster up.

"Thanks again for the ride, Max."

"No problem. I made a call and had your friends put on the list so they won't have any problems getting in."

"Thank you." I smiled big.

"My pleasure."

We pulled up to the club and Darren held out his hand to help me out. "Have fun in there and stay out of trouble." He gave a small smile.

"I can't make any promises." I winked.

I watched as Aria grabbed Max's hand and they cut in front of me to get into the club first. Whatever. She was a skank in a skintight white dress that showed the outline of her thong. The only reason I noticed was because her ass looked mega huge. I stepped into the club and sent a text message to Hannah, asking where she was.

"Sitting at a table to the left of the bar."

The blaring bass of the music was causing the floor underneath my feet to shake. Bodies that tangled all over the dance floor crowded the new club. Aria dragged Max over to the bar and I took off to find Hannah and Austin.

"There you are!" Hannah smiled as I sat down next to her. "You look hot!"

"Thanks." I reached across the table and shook the hand of Dominic, Austin's boyfriend.

Before I knew it, Max sat down in the empty seat next to me and handed me a mojito.

"I figured you'd want one. Reminds me of another time." He winked.

"Everyone, I'd like you to meet my friend, Max Hamilton, and his friend, Aria."

Hannah had the same reaction on her face as I did the first time I saw him. "Oh my God, Emma. He's so fucking hot."

I gently smiled at her and took a sip of my drink. Aria stood up and grabbed Max's hand, leading him to the dance floor. I sat there and watched as that slut moved her body up and down Max, grinding to the beat of the music. I touched the arm of the waitress that walked by and asked her to get us a round of lemon shots. I wasn't about to sit here and watch the two of them sober.

Downing two rounds of lemon shots, the effects of the alcohol mixed with the three mojitos started to take over. As soon as "Uptown Funk" blasted through the speakers, Hannah grabbed my hand and led me to the dance floor. I let loose, shaking my hips to the beat and moving my body around in a seductive way that suggested I was an easy target for sex. A tall and good-looking guy slithered in my direction, pressing his body up against mine as he smiled and our hips moved in sync. The final straw was when his hands grasped my waist and Max was near me in a flash, grabbing my wrist and leading me off the dance floor and through the club, to a hallway off to the side where nobody was allowed to go. He pushed me inside a small room, a room that was an office with a desk, a couch, and a couple of chairs. He turned on the light and slammed the door, locking it from within.

"What the fuck, Max?!"

"Shut up." His mouth crashed into mine as his hands went up the back of my dress, cupping my ass as hard as he could. He broke our kiss and his angered eyes stared into me. "Don't you ever do that again as long as we're engaged. Do you fucking understand me, Emma?"

I was stunned and shocked by his tone and his behavior and I didn't like it. The only reaction I could muster up was my hand slapping him across the face.

"Don't you ever, and I mean ever, fucking talk to me like that again! And don't you ever grab me like that again either. You have no right, you sorry son-of-a-bitch."

I stomped out of the room and quickly made my way down the hallway, sending a text message to Hannah telling her that I was sick and had to leave. My stomach was nauseous as I left the club and headed down a street that I wasn't familiar with. I didn't know where I was going and, at this point, I didn't care. Getting away from him was the only thing I wanted to do. I felt the vomit rise up in my throat as I stepped into the alley and bent over, releasing the alcohol that needed to escape me. A pair of hands lightly gripped my arms as I flinched.

"It's okay, Emma. It's me," Max whispered.

As soon as I was finished, he picked me up in his arms and carried me to the curb where Darren was waiting with the door open. He slid me in the back seat and I turned and faced the window.

"Emma," he spoke.

I put my hand up, signaling him not to say another word. Darren pulled up to my building and Max slid out, holding out his hand to help me. I pushed it away.

"I don't need your help." I heard him tell Darren that it was okay to leave and I abruptly stopped before reaching the door.

"Don't you dare follow me up to my apartment. You aren't welcome."

"You're making a scene, Emma. Let's just go upstairs and get some coffee."

I huffed and stumbled away from him. I couldn't find my keys, so Max found them for me and slid the key into the lock. As soon as I walked in, I kicked off my shoes and threw my purse down. The door shut and Max took hold of my arm, pulling me into him and brushing his lips against mine.

"I never got to tell you how fucking sexy you look in that dress," he spoke in between kisses.

A part of me was still angry at him for earlier, but the other part of me desired him inside of me. I kissed him hard, practically throwing myself at him to let him know that he could fuck me. A moan rumbled from his chest as he pulled down my panties and dipped his fingers inside of me while his mouth devoured my neck. My fingers raced to unbutton his pants and release his hard cock in my hand. As I slid his pants down, he stepped out of them and kicked them away while unzipping the back of my dress and letting it fall to the ground. His other hand grasped my breast and his fingers tugged at my hardened nipples. Max picked me up and set me down in front of the couch, turning me around so I was bent over. He didn't waste any time as he thrust inside of me, gripping my hips as moans escaped our lips. My body was heated and my heart was racing in sync with each thrust. His hand released my hip and his finger traveled down, circling my clit and sending my body into pure bliss as I began to climax. Yelling out his name, I gave in to my release as his thrusting slowed and he submerged himself deep into me while filling my insides. His hot breath trailed along my back as he moaned in erotic pleasure.

He pulled out of me and wrapped his arms around me, burying his face in my neck.

"Are you okay?" he asked, his voice soft and with bated breath.

"Yeah. I really want to go to bed."

He turned me around so I was facing him and picked me up, carrying me across the apartment and to my bedroom. He set me down and pulled back the covers.

"Would you like me to stay?"

I gave him a small smile and nodded my head as we both climbed into bed and he pulled me close to his body, where I fit perfectly.

Chapter 10

I opened my eyes as the sun filtered through the crack of the closed curtains. I noticed I was alone and couldn't remember if I told Max to stay the night. I could smell fresh coffee brewing, so I unsteadily climbed out of bed and slipped on a pair of panties and a t-shirt.

"Good morning, sunshine." Max smiled as he looked at what a hot mess I was.

I put my hand up to prevent him from speaking. "Lower your voice."

He chuckled. I took a seat on the stool at the counter as he handed me a cup of coffee and set a glass of orange juice in front of me.

"I'm making French toast. Would you like some?"

"Maybe one piece," I moaned as I leaned across the counter.

"Maybe you shouldn't drink so much and you wouldn't feel like shit."

"Oh please. Like you don't ever get drunk."

He smirked as he turned and looked at me. "You have a powerful hand."

Was I sorry that I slapped him? No. I wasn't. He deserved it. "Yeah, well, I have a powerful knee too if you want to try me."

"Ouch. That's not even funny." He lightly laughed.

I sat and stared at his muscular back as he cooked the French toast, daydreaming about running my tongue up and down his spine as the ends of my hair tickled his back. I sighed.

"You had no right last night, Max. You can't tell me what I can and can't do with other people. That's not how this works. We have an arrangement and that's all. If you want to change the agreement to where neither one of us sees other people for the next couple of months, let me know. Because the same rules apply to both of us, not just me. And by the way, what happened to Aria?"

He placed a piece of French toast on a plate and slid it to me. "I had Martin pick her up and take her home. She was pissed as hell."

"Then you should have stayed with her."

"Nah. I couldn't let you wander the streets of New York alone, especially at night and in your condition." He sat down next to me on the stool with his plate and began eating. "It's a deal."

"What's a deal?"

"No seeing other people until our arrangement is over. We're having sex now, so it won't be an issue."

Did he really just say that? Was that all he thought about? I rolled my eyes and attempted to eat.

"Are you sure you can commit to one woman for the next couple of months? Are you sure it won't be too difficult for you?"

He snickered at me. "You're cute when you're hung over." He finished his breakfast before I did and then grabbed his phone and called Darren to come pick him up.

"You're leaving?"

"Yeah. I have to get home and do some work. I have a meeting tomorrow morning and I'm not fully prepared. I want to get it done before dinner at my parents' house tonight."

"Ugh. I forgot about that."

He put his clothes on and kissed my forehead. "Take some aspirin. Drink plenty of fluids and rest up for tonight. I'll be by to pick you up around six o'clock and don't forget to put on your ring."

"I'll be ready and waiting."

"I'll see you later, babe." He walked out the door.

I grabbed my phone from my purse and sent a group message to Hannah and Austin.

Me: *"Sorry about last night. I wasn't feeling well."*

Austin: *"Don't worry about it. It happens."*

Hannah: *"Is something going on between you and Max? Because he looked really pissed when we were out there dancing and that guy came up to you."*

Me: *"We're sort of seeing each other."*

Austin: *"But he was with that girl last night."*

Me: *"Yeah, I know. I guess you can say that we made it official last night."*

Hannah: *"You're so lucky. He's so hot and rich. He's a keeper, Emma."*

Austin: *"Yeah. Don't let him get away."*

Me: *I'll see you two at school tomorrow. I have to do some things around the apartment and then I'm having dinner with Max and his parents later."*

****

Taking one last look in the mirror, I ran my fingers through my straightened blonde hair and dabbed on a light pink-colored lip-gloss. My phone started beeping with a text message and when I looked at it, it was from Macy.

"Hey, girl! Sorry I haven't been in touch. Service isn't the best over here. I hope you're all settled in and enjoying the apartment. I'll be home in a couple of weeks and we can spend enormous amounts of time catching up. Ciao."

I smiled but didn't send a message back due to the international charges. There was a knock on the door and, as usual, Max was right on time. When I opened it, Darren was standing there with a smile.

"Hello, Emma. You're looking better."

"Sorry about last night. It wasn't one of my finest moments." I grabbed my purse and shut the door.

"It's fine and I know Max can do that to you. I want to say congratulations for slapping him."

"He told you?"

"He tells me a lot of things and I'm sure he deserved it."

"That he did, Darren." I smiled.

We reached the Rolls Royce and I slid into the back seat. Max glanced at me and smiled as he held his phone up to his ear.

"I don't fucking care if they don't like it. You tell that son of a bitch if he doesn't agree to my terms, then he's out. Get back with me tomorrow."

He hung up and grabbed my hand, bringing it up to his lips. "You look gorgeous."

"Thanks. You're looking pretty spiffy yourself, Mr. Hamilton. Sounds like you're having an issue with someone."

"It's just work bullshit. I'll deal with it tomorrow."

"I talked to my mom today. It seems she's met someone."

"Good for her. Right?" He narrowed his eyes at me.

"I guess. As long as he's good to her."

Darren pulled up to the three-story red brick building with the little black wrought-iron gate in the front and opened the door. Stepping out, Darren opened the gate and held it as Max and I walked through. We walked up the four concrete steps that led to the door and, before we approached, the door opened and a small-framed woman in a maid's outfit stood there, welcoming us.

"Hello, Hattie."

"Hello, Mr. Hamilton. How are you this evening?"

She was a younger woman, I'd say about mid to late thirties with short black hair. I could tell by the look on her face she was smitten with Max.

"Hattie, this is Miss Knight."

"Please, call me Emma." I smiled at her.

"Your family is in the living room," she spoke as she shut the door behind us.

Max took hold of my hand and led me to the living room where his parents were properly seated in burgundy wingback chairs.

"Darling, it's so good to see you." Carol smiled as they hugged. "And Emma. You look as beautiful as ever."

"Can I get either of you a drink?" Bradshaw asked.

"Emma will have a glass of wine and I can get my own bourbon."

"A glass of wine for a beautiful young lady." Bradshaw smiled as he handed me the glass. I couldn't help but look at him with contempt for what he was doing behind his wife's back. Knowing what I knew had tainted my perception of him being a good man and a loving father.

"Thank you." I gave a small, non-deserving smile.

Hattie alerted us that dinner was ready and so we headed to the dining room.

"Where's Fiona?" Max asked.

"Right here, big brother." She smiled as she kissed him on the cheek. Her unfriendly eyes diverted my way and as she looked me up and down.

"Don't be rude, Fiona," Max stated.

"Hey." She walked around to the other side of the table and took the seat across from me.

"Our sweet little Fiona applied to Columbia today," Bradshaw proudly said.

"Good for you, sis."

"What do you want to study?" I asked.

"She's getting into law," Carol answered for her.

"My girlfriend is just finishing up her degree in law. She'll be graduating in December."

"Good for her. Where at? Miami?" She rolled her eyes. "And why the hell are you just starting Parsons anyway? Shouldn't you have been graduated already?"

"Fiona, that's enough." Max scowled.

"You're right, Fiona, but I chose not to go to college right from high school. I took a few years off to work."

"Stop right there, Emma." Max commanded. "It's none of Fiona's business."

The air was thick in the room and I didn't know what Fiona's problem with me was. Both times I'd seen her, she had been nothing but rude. We finished dinner and had dessert. Max poured me another glass of wine and leaned down and kissed my lips.

"Aw, look at those two lovebirds. They're perfect together." Carol smiled at us.

I felt bad for this charade. They were genuinely happy that their only son had finally found someone to settle down with. Little did they know that it wasn't going to last.

Chapter 11

It was Wednesday night and Max and I were having dinner together at my apartment. It was the first time I'd seen him since dinner with his parents on Sunday. I was making lasagna and waiting for him to come by after the office. As I was in the kitchen making the salad, the door opened, and Max walked in and set his briefcase down on the stool.

"Hi." I smiled.

"Hey. It smells delicious in here. How was school today?"

"It was good. How was work?"

"Hectic and stressful as always." He walked behind me and wrapped his arms around my waist, burying his face into my neck. "It's good to see you."

"It's good to see you too."

"Can I help?" he asked.

"Yes. Finish cutting up these tomatoes for the salad while I check on the lasagna." I reached up and kissed his soft lips before pulling the dish out of the oven.

Just as the two of us sat down at the table, there was a knock at the door.

"Are you expecting someone?"

"No. I have no idea who it could be."

"I'll answer it." He got up from the table and opened the door. My eyes widened and my heart started racing when I peeked over the table and saw Molly and Kara standing there.

"Umm. Is Emma here?"

"Yeah. Come on in, ladies."

I jumped up from the table and ran to them. "What are you doing here?" I asked as the three of us hugged.

"We wanted to surprise you, but I think you may have surprised us. Isn't that the guy from the club in Miami?"

I sighed.

"Yes, I am. I'm Max Hamilton." He held out his hand. "We were never formally introduced."

"What's going on, Emma?" Molly asked.

I stood there and stared at my best friends from whom I never kept a secret. I didn't expect this visit and they caught me off guard.

"Come sit down and have some lasagna. I'll explain everything, but first let me pour you a drink because you're going to need it."

Max and I explained everything to them and I could tell they weren't happy about the situation. The two of them glared at me from across the table, a glare that I came to know growing up. After dinner, Max helped clean up and then said his goodbyes to Molly and Kara.

"It was lovely to finally meet the two of you officially this time." He winked. He placed his thumb on my chin. "You owe me sex."

"I know. Sorry." I pouted.

"It's all good. I'm glad your friends are here. Go catch up and I'll talk to you tomorrow."

He walked out the door and as soon as I shut it, the girls were right behind me, grabbing my arms and dragging me to the couch.

"What the fuck, Emma? How the hell are you going to pull this off?" Kara asked with concern.

"It's easy. After he collects his trust fund, I'm breaking off the engagement."

"That's not what she meant," Molly chimed.

I looked at both of them as I narrowed one eye. "What are you talking about?"

"I can already tell you're falling in love with him if you aren't already in love with him. I've never seen you like this before. You're different. I saw it in the way you looked at him every time he spoke."

"You're going to get hurt, Emma, and we're worried for you." Molly put her arm around me.

"You're both wrong. I don't love Max. This is an agreement we have. There's no love between us. Only amazing sex and friendship. We're the friends-with-benefits couple and nothing else. I don't have time for love or relationships and neither does he."

"If you say so, but we're still worried," Kara spoke.

I grabbed the bottle of wine from the table and brought it over to the couch with our glasses. "Now, tell me why the two of you are here."

Excitement overtook both of them at the same time as their faces displayed huge smiles.

"We're moving to New York!" Kara screamed.

"You're kidding, right? Because seriously, that's not even funny if you're joking."

Molly took hold of my hand. "No, Emma. We aren't kidding around. We both have interviews tomorrow at a new hair salon that's opening up over on Madison Avenue. They're looking to hire ten new stylists. We miss you and Miami hasn't been the same since you left and you know we've always wanted to see New York."

I could barely contain my excitement. Having my best friends, who were like sisters to me, with me in New York was like a dream come true. I missed them so much and the fun times we used to have.

"Poor Aubrey. Now she's going to be left all alone back in Miami."

Molly looked at me and gave me a big smile. "We were waiting for the best piece of news for last. She's moving to New York too!"

"WHAT?!" I screamed in excitement.

"After she graduates in December, she has a job waiting for her at Lawson, Talbot, and Grimes Law Firm. She did a Skype interview with them and they hired her. She wanted to come here with us and tell you in person, but with her classes, she couldn't."

I started jumping up and down because I was so happy. Then reality hit me. "What if you two don't get the job at the salon?"

"We already thought of that and it doesn't matter. We'll find jobs at one of these salons in New York or even Jersey." Kara smiled.

****

Kara and Molly stayed the night. I had to get up and go to class, so I left the extra key on the counter for them. As I walked to class, I dialed Aubrey.

"Hello, my dearest best friend," she answered.

"I can't believe you're moving to New York in December and didn't tell me!"

She laughed. "I wanted to, but the other two goofballs wanted to do it in person. I'm so excited, Emma, and I'm ready to make a fresh start."

"I am thrilled that we're all going to be together. I just got to class, so I'll talk to you later. Love you, Aubrey."

"Love you too, girly!"

I couldn't wait to introduce Hannah and Austin to my friends, as I was telling them all about the girls. During my last class, a text message came through from Max.

"Dinner tonight. The four of us. I'll pick you ladies up at seven o'clock and then you're spending the night at my house. So pack a bag."

"What if I don't want to spend the night?"

"It's not an option. You owe me sex and I'm ready to collect."

I smiled and rolled my eyes. *"See you at seven."*

He was becoming the most important person in my life very quickly. I knew that falling in love with him wasn't an option, but it was too late and I knew he was falling for me. The question was: how were we going to continue our relationship after he collected his trust fund?

When I arrived home and opened the door, Molly and Kara were huddled on the couch, watching *Sex in the City* with a pint of ice cream in their hands and two spoons. I set my purse down and sat in between them.

"How did your interviews go?"

"Great," Kara spoke. "They said they'd let us know by the end of tomorrow."

"I'm keeping my fingers crossed for both of you! By the way, Max is picking us up at seven for dinner." I took the spoon from Kara and dipped it in the ice cream.

"Please tell me he has a brother," Molly begged.

"Sorry. He only has a nasty seventeen-year-old sister named Fiona. For some reason, that girl hates me."

"Friends, perhaps?" Kara smiled.

"I never met any of his friends."

"That's weird. Don't you think you should?"

I shrugged. "We have a three-month arrangement. He probably doesn't want his friends involved."

I took one last bite of ice cream and got up from the couch to change for dinner. Kara and Molly followed to do the same. At precisely seven o'clock, there was a knock on the door. When I opened it, Darren was standing there.

"Come on in, Darren. We're almost ready."

"Max informed me that your friends were in town and that you were forced to tell them about your 'arrangement.'"

"Yeah. But I trust them with my life, so I'm not worried. Molly. Kara. I would like you to meet Darren, Max's driver."

"Nice to meet you, ladies." Darren smiled.

"Nice to meet you too, Darren," they both chimed at the same time.

We walked down to the car and I looked around because the only thing in front of the building was a limousine.

"No Rolls today, Darren?"

"Not today, Emma." He winked as he opened the door.

I slid in first, taking the seat next to Max. "Hey, good looking." I smiled as I leaned over and kissed his lips.

"Hey, beautiful." He took my bag from me and set it down on the floor. "Hello, ladies."

Both girls blushed as they sat across from us. It wasn't hard to do when one of the hottest and sexiest guys in the universe spoke to you.

"Did you tell them about the engagement party?"

"Umm. No."

"We would love if the two of you would join us Saturday night at our engagement party."

Molly frowned. "Engagement party? Isn't that taking things a bit far?"

"It's my parents. They feel the need to show off to their friends."

"We'd love to come and celebrate your fake engagement."
Kara smiled.

We drank, talked, and laughed as we ate dinner and I
couldn't have been more pleased at how well Max got along
with my friends. I had visions of a future where we'd be sitting
here with Kara and Molly and their boyfriends, laughing and
having a good time. I had to have a little hope that when all was
said and done at the end of three months, Max would love me
enough to want to keep me in his life. After a great dinner and
conversation, we dropped the girls back at my apartment and I
went home with Max where our first round of sex took place in
the kitchen because we couldn't make it up to the bedroom fast
enough.

Chapter 12

"Good morning," Max whispered as he kissed the side of my head.

My hand ran down the front of his torso as I curled up closer to him, not wanting to leave his bed or his side. Our night of passion topped it all and my body was still reeling in the effects of the things he did to me.

"Do you have to go to work?"

"Unfortunately, I do. I have a meeting first thing. You don't have classes today, so what are your plans?" His finger made tiny circles around my shoulder, sending me into a frenzy.

"I'm going to show the girls around New York and then go shopping. I need to get a dress for our engagement party tomorrow."

"I'll give Melanie a call over at Bergdorf's and tell her to expect you. Whatever you find, put it on my account and don't be shy about it. Understand me?"

I looked up at him with a smile as I traced the outline of his lips. "Yes. I'll go see Melanie at Bergdorf's."

"Good. Now let me have that pussy before I get ready for work." He rolled over and dipped his fingers inside me, ensuring that I was ready for him. And I was. I was always ready when he was around.

****

"You must be Emma," the tall redhead spoke. "Max described you to a tee."

"And you must be Melanie."

"If you ladies would like to come with me, I've pulled some dresses for you all to try on."

"Us?" Kara asked in shock.

"Yes. Max said the three of you will be needing dresses for an event tomorrow."

Molly grabbed my arm. "He's buying us dresses too?"

"I guess so."

"I think I'm officially in love with him," Kara swooned.

I put up the hand with my engagement ring on it. "Back off, bitches. He's mine." I laughed.

I tried on the first couple of dresses and sent a picture to Max, asking what he thought.

"What do you think of this one?"

"I'm not sure. Why don't you step outside the dressing room and show me."

My belly fluttered at the thought that he was right outside the dressing room. I pulled back the curtain and stepped out, only to find Max sitting in the chair, staring at me.

"What are you doing here? I thought you had to work?"

"I had a few moments to spare, so I thought I'd come here and see what you girls were up to."

"Well?" I asked as I did a little spin.

"It looks great on you, but I don't think it's the right dress for the party."

I walked back into the dressing room and slipped into a long, off-white silk strapless gown embellished with beads around the waistline and knew instantly it was the one. I smiled before stepping out and showing Max.

"Wow. You look sexy as fuck in that dress." He smiled.

Molly and Kara took one look at me and their mouths dropped. "That's the one, Emma."

"I know. I do love it."

Max got up from the chair and walked over to me, placing his hand on my waist and kissing my cheek. "I have to go. I love that dress. I'll talk to you later."

"Are we hanging out tonight?" I asked.

"Nah. You spend the night with your friends. I'll see you tomorrow."

"Okay," I said with a bit of sadness. I sighed as he walked away.

I couldn't help but feel a twinge of pain inside because I so badly wanted to see him later. Not only for sex because my body craved his, but because I loved spending time with him. Molly and Kara found the perfect dresses and Melanie was going to have them delivered to the apartment tomorrow morning.

"Are you seeing Max tonight?" Kara asked.

"No. He told me to hang with you guys and he'll see me tomorrow."

"So what should we do tonight? It's a Friday night in New York City." Molly smiled.

Kara had her nose buried in her phone as she let out a small scream. "How far is Bowery Ballroom from your apartment?"

"I don't know. Why?"

"Guess who's playing there tonight?"

"Who?" Molly asked in suspense.

"High Five!"

"Shut the fuck up! That indie band from Miami?"

"Yes! Looks like we're going to see them tonight, ladies!" Molly expressed.

"The lead singer, Lucas, is so hot. I think he had a thing for you, Emma."

"He did not." I waved my hand.

Kara hooked her arm in mine. "So him buying you every drink that night in Miami didn't mean anything?"

"Please. I'm sure he buys all the girls drinks."

"He didn't buy ours." Molly frowned.

****

Getting ready to go out, Kara squealed as her phone rang. It was the salon calling. After hanging up, she jumped up and down, saying she got the job, and they wanted her to start in two weeks. Not too long after, Molly received the same call.

"This calls for some serious celebrating tonight!" Kara announced.

I was so excited that my friends had secured jobs and they would moving to New York City. I pulled out my phone and sent a text message to Max.

"Guess what? Molly and Kara got the jobs at the salon!"

I set my phone down and finished doing my hair and makeup. He never replied. I slipped into my slim-fitting black jeans and my new black embellished trapeze cami. As I took one last look in the mirror, I put on my black four-inch heel strappy sandals and grabbed my clutch, ready to let loose to the music from the band, High Five.

As the cab dropped us off in front of the Bowery Ballroom, we stepped inside and took note of the crowd of people hovering in front of the stage, waiting for the show to start. Off to the side was a private seating area where I saw a familiar face. Ugh, it was Fiona. She stood up when she saw me and walked over.

"Hey," she spoke.

"Hey, Fiona. I would like you to meet my friends, Molly and Kara. This is Max's sister, Fiona."

Surprisingly, she gave them a friendly smile and then proceeded to ask me a question.

"You like High Five?"

"Yeah. We saw them a couple of times in Miami. Great band."

"They're one of my favorites. I can't believe you know of them. That's pretty cool."

"If you play your cards right, little sister, maybe Emma can introduce you to the lead singer." Molly smiled.

"What? You know Lucas Wayne?"

"We talked a few times after the shows back in Miami."

"Oh my God. That is so awesome. Hey, there's an extra table next to mine if you'd like to sit there."

"You mean in the private section?" I asked in confusion as to why she was suddenly being so nice.

"Yeah. When I found out they were coming to New York, I reserved a couple of tables. The Hamilton name can get you anything."

"Thanks, Fiona. That's very sweet of you."

We followed her to the black table and chairs that sat on the side of the stage.

"Best seats in the house." She smiled.

She introduced me to her posse and she picked up a glass of wine.

"You're not twenty-one. How did you get that?"

"Like I said, the Hamilton name can get you anything."

Kara, Molly, and I took our seats at the next table and ordered our own drinks. Fiona and her friends looked way older than seventeen and it made me wonder if her parents or Max knew she was here. As Kara and Molly got up to go find the restroom, Fiona sat down next to me.

"Hey, I'm sorry I've been such a bitch to you. I know your engagement to Max is fake and I didn't want to like you and then you disappear."

I was stunned. "Our engagement isn't fake. Why would you say that?"

"I'm not stupid, Emma. I know my brother, and he will never settle down. He's doing this to get his trust fund."

"I don't know what you're talking about." I began to get nervous.

"It's okay. I won't say anything to anyone, and if he truly loved you and was going to marry you, why would he have taken Christine to the ballet tonight?"

I couldn't comprehend what she had said because a feeling of hurt washed over me. "He went to the ballet tonight?"

"You didn't know?" She pulled out her phone and showed me a picture she secretly took of the two of them leaving his apartment building. He was dressed in a tux and she was in a long red gown.

"Does he know you took that?"

"No. I had Lizzy's driver stop by there on the way here so I could pick up a bracelet that I'd left there a couple of weeks ago, and that's when I saw him and Christine leaving. I saw the tickets sitting on his kitchen counter and I assumed he was taking you."

"So who is this Christine?" I asked.

"A girl he's dated on and off. I'm sorry, Emma."

I put on my fake smile. "Don't be sorry. You're right, I'm doing Max a favor and, in return, he's helping me out. Please don't tell anyone and please don't tell him you saw me here tonight."

"I won't. Don't worry and your secret is safe with me. I love my brother and I hate what my parents have done to make him do this. Max is an amazing guy and brother, but he just can't settle for one girl. I guess you could say he takes after our dad. I'm sure he's told you about my dad's affairs."

"Yeah. He's mentioned it."

Kara and Molly arrived back at the table just in time for the opening band to start playing. Fiona went back to her table and I sat there, upset and jealous that Max took that girl to the ballet instead of me. He broke our rule of not seeing anyone until our engagement was over. That sorry son of a bitch. Now I was pissed as hell. I slipped my ring off my finger and put it in my purse.

The opening band ended and, finally, High Five took the stage. We all stood up from our seats in the private seating area and started shouting and waving our hands. Wow, did Lucas look good up there. He had on a pair of dark wash jeans and a black muscle shirt that showed off his muscular arms. His brown hair, which had once been longer, was now cut short on the sides with a longer top that he swept over to the side, enhancing his already dreamy brown eyes. He ran across the stage as he sang the first song. Once the song was over, he and the band talked to the crowd, telling us how awesome New York City is. Fiona stood on her chair and screamed his name. When he turned to look at her, his eyes met mine and a wide smile splayed across his face. He pointed at me and winked. Molly reached over and grabbed my arm in excitement.

"This next song is a song I wrote after spending a few hours with a girl named Emma. It's called "Whoever She Is." He strummed his guitar. The crowd went crazy. Fiona ran over to me.

"Oh my effin' God! That is one of my favorite songs and he wrote that about you!" she screamed.

I took the last sip of my mojito as he sang the rest of the song. Ten songs later and their performance was finally over. As soon as they exited off the stage, one of the security guys walked up to me.

"Are you Emma?"

"Yes."

"Lucas would like to see you in the back. He said to bring your friends too."

"Here we go again." Kara smiled.

I looked over at Fiona, who had practically stopped breathing, and hooked my arm around her. "Wanna hang out with us?"

"Really?" she asked in excitement.

"Yeah." I smiled as we were led to the back of the lounge and into a large room.

When we walked through the door, Lucas turned and looked at me.

"Hello, Emma."

"Hello, Lucas. You remember my friends Kara and Molly?"

"Of course. Wasn't there one more?"

I laughed. "Yeah. That would be Aubrey. She's back in Miami. I would love for you to meet my friend, Fiona Hamilton. She's a huge fan."

He took her hand and brought it up to his lips, giving it a soft kiss. I thought Fiona was going to pass out.

"It's a pleasure to meet you, Fiona. Would you ladies like to join us down on the first level for a few drinks? On me, of course."

We followed the band down to the first level, where we were seated at a large table. Lucas signaled for the bartender, ordering us a round of drinks for the adults and cokes for Fiona and her friends.

"What a surprise seeing you here in New York, Emma."

"I live here now. I'm attending Parsons School of Design."

"Very cool." He smiled.

We sat and talked for a couple of hours and, a few drinks later, I was really feeling the alcohol.

"Would you like to come back to the hotel with us?"

The offer was tempting and, for a split second, I thought about it. If Max could break the rules, then so could I.

"She's engaged to my brother," Fiona proudly spoke.

Lucas looked at me and tilted his head. "You're engaged?"

Thank you, Fiona. "Yeah." I looked down.

"Where's your ring?"

I reached in my purse, pulled it out, and then slipped it on my finger. "It's a little big and I didn't want to lose it."

He narrowed his eyes at me as his lips slowly parted. "I see."

God, he was sexy and I could see Fiona swooning over him and his band members.

"How would you like to perform at Emma and Max's engagement party tomorrow night?" Fiona asked.

I just about had a heart attack as I shot her a look. *What the fuck was she doing?*

"We charge a fee for performance," Lucas said.

"Whatever your fee is, I'll pay double." She smiled.

"How old are you?" Lucas slyly asked.

"I'm seventeen, soon to be eighteen, and I'm very wealthy, so money isn't a problem."

Lucas looked at her with a grin on his face. "I think we'd love to perform tomorrow. Give me the address and time and we'll be there."

Great. Fuck me right now. "We have to go, Lucas. Thank you for tonight." I got up and grabbed Fiona by the arm. "Let's go."

"See you tomorrow, Emma." He winked.

We walked out the doors and I stopped and looked at Fiona. "What the hell do you think you're doing?"

"What? They're a great band and you love them, so why shouldn't they play at your engagement party? Think about it, Emma. It would piss my parents off to no end and think of Max's reaction. Wouldn't you love to get a rise out of him, especially after taking Christine to the ballet tonight instead of you, his fiancée?"

"I don't play games like that, Fiona."

"I do, and trust me, this will be good." Before she stepped into her limo, she turned and looked at me. "By the way, this so-called engagement is a game." She climbed in and shut the door.

Molly hailed us a cab and Kara put her hand on my shoulder. "That girl is something else for a seventeen-year-old. You better watch out for her."

I sighed as we rode back to the apartment.

Chapter 13

Fuck. Another hangover plagued me as I opened my eyes to my phone beeping. I reached over and grabbed it, noticing a text message from Max.

"Where the fuck were you last night and who the hell is that guy you're with? My sister posted a pic of you and him on Instagram."

Wow. Really, Max? He goes to the ballet with some skank and he has the nerve to question me? As angry as I was, I didn't want to start an argument with him on the day of our engagement party. I didn't owe him an explanation. It was none of his fucking business where I was or what I did. He broke the rules, not me. I didn't reply. About an hour later, there was knock on the front door. Shit. I knew it was him. I climbed out of bed in my silk nightshirt and stumbled across the apartment. As soon as I opened the door, Max came barreling in.

"You didn't answer my text message!" he shouted.

"Will you be quiet? The girls are still asleep."

He stood there, looking sexy as fuck and slowly shaking his head at me. The anger that consumed me was quickly being replaced by my desire for him. *Shit. Shit. Shit.* I knew what was about to happen. I could see the hunger in his eyes.

"Damn you, Emma." He walked over to me and smashed his mouth into mine, cupping each side of my face with his hands. I jumped up and wrapped my legs around him as he held me up and carried me to the bedroom, kicking the door shut with his foot. He lay me on the bed and I scooted up, laying my head on the pillow as he pulled his shirt over his head and his jeans off, kicking them to the side. He stood at the end of the bed and reached up under my nightshirt, grabbing the sides of my panties and pulling them down. My eyes closed as his tongue slid up my inner thigh, teasing me and begging for more as the warmth of his breath enveloped my aching sweet spot that was filled with lust and desire for him. The wetness of his lips grazed over my clit as his fingers imprisoned my insides. Soft, sweet moans escaped him as his mouth pleasured me beyond words. The buildup was happening as my hands planted themselves on each side of his face, holding him down there until I climaxed. As much as I wanted to scream from the gratification of his talented mouth, I couldn't because of Molly and Kara. My body tightened as my release came and I threw my head back in delight. His tongue embarked on a journey up my torso while his hands pushed up my nightshirt, exposing my breasts. Grasping the left one with his hand, his mouth worshiped my entire right breast before his lips clamped around my hardened peak, nibbling and suckling before he moved over to the next one.

I wanted to touch him and feel his hardness in my hand before he fucked me. He scooted up closer so his mouth was hovering over mine as he looked into my eyes before softly kissing me. Reaching down and taking hold of his cock, I moved my hand firmly up and down his length as he gasped while I ran my thumb over the slickness of his engorged head.

"I want you to ride me," he whispered as he rolled over and pulled me on top of him, slowly pushing himself inside of me.

I inhaled deeply as I sat up, driving him deeper inside of me. His fingers took hold of the bottom of my nightshirt and he slowly lifted it over my head, exposing my entire naked body to his eyes. As I moved in small, tight motions on his cock, his hands kneaded my breasts and tugged at my nipples before he pulled me down and took them in his mouth. The buildup was happening as I sat up and planted my hand firmly on his chest while I circled my hips and then moved back and forth, causing him to throw his head back. Grabbing my hips and holding me in place, he lifted himself and thrust in and out of me as fast as he could, sending me to the peak of another orgasm. Panting, and with my heart racing, I released myself on him as he released himself inside of me, pushing deeper with one last long stroke. I collapsed on top him and he wrapped his arms around me, holding me tight.

As our breathing calmed, I rolled off of him and turned on my side, facing him, stroking his bare muscular chest. He looked at me and kissed my head, lifting his arm up around me and pulling me into him.

"I want to know where you were last night," he spoke.

I lifted myself out of his grip and got up and put on a new pair of panties. "How was your date with Christine?" I asked as I slipped on my nightshirt.

He placed his hands behind his head and glared at me.

"How was the ballet, Max?"

As I stared at him from the end of the bed, he bit his bottom lip. "How did you know?"

"It doesn't matter how I knew. You broke our agreement." I walked out of the bedroom and headed to the kitchen for some coffee. He followed behind in only his jeans. Kara and Molly were sitting at the table, staring at us. I watched as their mouths dropped to the floor as they stared at Max.

"Don't get smart with me. Who was that guy?"

"And who the fuck is Christine?!" I yelled in his face.

Kara and Molly got up. "We'll leave you two alone so you can argue in peace."

I rolled my eyes as Max said good morning to them.

"You ditched me last night so you could take another woman to the ballet. You suck, Max. You really suck!"

He poured himself some coffee, because I refused to get him some, and sat down on the stool. "I'm sorry, Emma. I bought the tickets before I met you and I told her that I'd take her. What kind of man would I be to suddenly tell her that I changed my mind?"

"The fucking kind of man who has the balls to tell her that he has a fiancée!"

"Why would I do that? It's not even a real engagement. Now who was that guy you were with and why were you with my sister?"

I didn't feel like I owed him any explanation at all, but I couldn't stand arguing with him anymore, so I caved.

"His name is Lucas and he's the lead singer of a band from Miami called High Five. We had seen them a couple of times in Miami and, after the show, we chatted. When we found out they were playing last night, we went and your sister was there with her girlfriends. She showed me the picture of you and Christine. Apparently, she left her bracelet at your apartment and when she stopped by to get it, she saw you coming out of the building with her. And by the way, she knows our engagement isn't real."

"What? What the fuck!" he yelled.

"Don't worry about her. She won't tell your parents because she feels sorry for you. Anyway, your sister loves the band and I introduced her to them. We all sat around after the show and we talked. Your sister must have taken our picture, but I don't remember her doing it."

He looked away from me as his jaw moved back and forth. He was so angry but had no right to be.

"Did you fuck her last night?" I boldly asked.

His eyes looked into mine as he cocked his head. "Did you fuck him last night?"

"No, because I'm not a whore. Contrary to what you might believe, Mr. Hamilton. Now, if you'll excuse me, I want you to leave my apartment!"

"I didn't fuck her, Emma. I just took her to the ballet. I was home by eleven o'clock, alone."

"You know what, Max. I don't give a rat's ass anymore what you do. We have two more months of this arrangement. Let's just try to be civil to each other long enough to get through it."

"Why are you so upset? Just explain that to me," he softly spoke.

"Because you lied to me. You didn't tell me where you were going or that you'd be going with another woman. We had an agreement not to see other people as long as we were in this so-called fake relationship."

"I'm sorry. I didn't mean to lie to you. But this is the exact reason why I can't be tied down in a relationship. Nobody tells me what I can and can't do. I'm the only one who makes that decision. No one else."

My heart ached something fierce and tears filled my eyes. I couldn't let him see me about to cry over him. I wouldn't give him the power or the satisfaction.

"You're right, Max, and I apologize. The same goes for me. No one will ever question what I do. I will never allow it."

He walked over and wrapped his arms around me from behind, burying his face into my neck. "I'm sorry. I don't want to argue with you. I'll be by to pick you up around six o'clock for the party, okay?"

I nodded my head.

He pressed his lips against my neck and walked into the bedroom to gather the rest of his clothes and then walked out the door while I stood looking out the window.

"Are you okay?" Molly asked with concern.

"What the fuck did I get myself into?" I broke down and all the tears that I held back when Max was here suddenly fell down my face.

Kara walked over and hugged me. "You were doing it for the right reason. You didn't expect to fall in love with him."

"How can anyone not fall in love with him? I mean, look at him, for fuck sake. Every time he's near me, I have an orgasm."

Molly and Kara both laughed. "I think we know what you mean. He obviously has some deep issues, Emma, which stem from his father and his behavior. I know you don't want to hear this, but I think it's best that you don't get any further involved with him. He can't be saved unless he wants to be and, from the sounds of it, he doesn't want to be."

I swallowed hard because everything Kara said was true, but if he didn't have feelings for me, then why did he act like that over Lucas?

"I'm going back to bed. I'm too tired to deal with the subject of Max anymore." I walked back to my room and climbed into the bed that smelled like him and pulled the covers over me.

Fuck! I climbed out of bed and grabbed the throw that sat on the chair in my room and took it out to the couch. Kara and Molly were in the kitchen.

"I thought you were going to bed?" Molly asked.

"I can't sleep in that bed with his smell all over it." I pulled the throw over me as I lay down on the couch and fell asleep.

Chapter 14

Molly finished putting the final touches on my hair as I looked at the clock. It was five minutes until six o'clock.

"There. Now slip into that beautiful dress." She smiled.

I went to my closet and pulled out the dress that was delivered earlier while I was sleeping. It looked just as beautiful as it did yesterday. Just as I put it on, there was a knock at the door.

"Can one of you get that? It's Darren. Tell him I'll be ready soon."

As I slipped my feet into my new shoes, Max walked into the bedroom.

"My God, you look beautiful." He smiled as I turned around.

My heart started racing from nerves because of our fight this morning, and I wasn't quite ready to see him yet. "Thanks." I turned away.

"I bought you something." Max walked over and handed me a long blue velvet box.

"You shouldn't have."

"Just open it, Emma."

As I took the box from his hand, I noticed it was from Tiffany's. I lifted the top and inside sat a beautiful diamond butterfly pendant on a silver chain.

"Max. It's beautiful."

He took the box from my hands and removed the necklace from it, placing it around my neck as I stared in the mirror.

"The butterfly is a symbol of transformation. We all have different stages in our life where we transform and, in order to get to the next stage, we have to go through changes that will shape us into who we will be next. She represents faith, and as she flits among the flowers, she dances. I always want you to dance, Emma. Promise me you'll never stop dancing."

Chills ran up and down my spine as he spoke and a tear filled my eye. "Thank you, Max. It's truly beautiful."

He turned me around and swept the back of his hand across my cheek. "I'm sorry about earlier. I didn't mean to be such a dick."

"Apology accepted."

He leaned down and brushed his lips against mine. "We better get going or my mom is going to go into a fit of rage if we're late."

The four of us climbed into the limo that Martin was driving.

"Where's Darren?" I whispered in Max's ear.

"He has the night off." He winked.

We arrived at his parents' house and as soon as we walked in, everyone began to clap.

"There they are!" Carol exclaimed. "Our happy little couple has finally arrived."

I smiled as she and Bradshaw gave me a light hug and introduced them to Kara and Molly. The house was filled with floral arrangements of white dahlias and pink roses. Soft music was playing in every room and guests were mixing and mingling amongst each other. Max grabbed a glass of champagne from the waiter that passed by and handed it to me.

"You are simply stunning. I love that dress." Carol smiled as she grabbed my hands and held them. "Come on. I'm anxious to show you off to all my friends."

After meeting a room full of people that I'd never see again, Fiona walked up to me and tapped me on the shoulder.

"They'll be here soon." She smiled. "I'm so excited I can barely stand it."

"Who will be here soon?" Max asked as he looked at his sister.

"You'll see." She smirked and walked away.

"What the fuck is she up to?"

I wasn't about to get in the middle of that one, so I graciously excused myself to the bathroom. As I walked down the hallway, I heard moaning noises coming from the room across from the bathroom. If I remembered correctly, it was Bradshaw's office. After I finished in the bathroom and opened the door, I was startled by the woman that opened the door across the hall. She stopped and her eyes widened when she saw me. I happened to glance over her shoulder and I could see Bradshaw buttoning up his pants. I looked down and continued to walk back to where all the guests were. Max took hold of my arm and whispered in my ear.

"Your band has arrived."

"They aren't my band and I had nothing to do with it. Your sister paid for them to play here tonight."

Max walked away with an anger in his eyes and I was completely confused as to what the fuck was going on in his head. I grabbed another glass of champagne as I shook it off and found Kara, Molly, and Fiona talking to Lucas.

"Well, hello there, pretty lady." He smiled as he looked me up and down.

Max walked up behind me and wrapped his arms around me. "Hey, baby."

"Max, I would like you to meet Lucas, lead singer of High Five."

"Hey. You're a very lucky man to be marrying this beautiful woman. We met back in Miami."

"I know I am. I fell in love with her from the moment I saw her."

"Not hard to do, man."

This was awkward and I was very uncomfortable. Suddenly, Bradshaw called for everyone's attention.

"Carol and I would like to make a toast to the future Mr. and Mrs. Hamilton. We are so proud that our son has finally found the love of his life and wants to settle down. Much like I have the love of my life standing by my side. We have created a beautiful family and a successful family business, and we couldn't ask for anything more. Emma is lovely and I do believe my son has made an outstanding choice. To Max and Emma. May your love be as eternal as ours is."

I wanted to throw up. Actually, I felt like I could have at that moment. That man was so full of bullshit he made my stomach turn. I looked over to the left and noticed the girl that I saw coming out of his office watching him.

"Who is that girl over there with the blonde hair?" I asked Max.

"That's Rosalina, one of the interns at the office. Why?"

"Is she the *one*?" I asked, even though I knew the answer.

"No. Michelle isn't here tonight."

I'll be damned. He's screwing two interns. I didn't want to say anything to Max because he was upset enough about Michelle.

"Why did you ask about Rosalina?"

"No reason. She just keeps staring at me. That's all."

Max leaned closer to my ear. "Maybe she thinks you're hot."

"Maybe we could have a threesome," I whispered back.

"You would actually do that?"

I placed my hand on his chest. "Only in your dreams, Max."

The band began to play and I could see the excitement bursting out of Fiona.

"I saw the way he looked at you," Max spoke.

"Who?"

"Lucas. I think he wants you."

"I think he does too. He certainly made no secret about it back in Miami. I think once our engagement has come to an end, I'll give him a call."

I could see the anger wash over Max's face. "He'll use you."

"Isn't that what you're doing?" I walked away with a grin on my face.

Max took hold of my arm and led me inside the house.

"What are you doing?"

"You'll see." He took me upstairs to his old bedroom and shut the door, locking it behind him. He grabbed my wrists and held them above my head as his mouth crashed into mine and I fell back against the wall. His kiss was feral and exciting but full of anger.

"Do you want me to fuck you up against this wall?"

I stared into his beautiful eyes as he stared back, waiting for my answer. I swallowed hard.

"Yes."

"Are you sure? Or do you want *him* to fuck you?"

"You."

"Say it," he growled as he lifted my dress, pulled down my panties, and then unbuttoned his pants, letting them fall down to his ankles.

"I want you to fuck me right now."

My dress was getting in the way, so he let go of my wrists and turned me around so he could unzip it. As soon as it fell to the ground, he turned me around, leaning against me and pinning my wrists above my head with one hand.

"I wanted to fuck you from behind, but then I wouldn't be able to watch you bite that beautiful lip when I make you come all over me."

He thrust deep and hard inside of me and I gasped. He brought my leg up around his waist as he moved sharply in and out of me, moaning in pleasure. I lifted my other leg and wrapped them both around him as he let go of my wrists and held me up while he pounded into me like an animal, bringing me to a magnificent orgasm.

"That's right, baby. Come for me and only me. I know you love it when I fuck you like this."

His lips brushed over mine as he pushed deeper inside me and filled me up with his come. "For now, you're mine," he whispered in my ear.

He set me down and pulled out of me, bending down and pulling up his pants. He handed me my panties and my dress.

"We better get back out there before people notice we're gone and come looking for us."

I slipped on my panties and my dress and asked him to zip me up.

"Would it be so bad that they knew we just fucked in your room? After all, isn't perception everything?" I wiped my lips and walked out of the bedroom. From this day forth, I wasn't going to play the emotion game anymore. Max Hamilton wanted nothing more than a physical relationship and that was what he was going to get. It was time I prepared myself for the day he walked out of my life.

Chapter 15

"I'm going to miss you," I whined as I hugged Molly and Kara at the airport.

"We'll be back in less than two weeks and then the hunt is on for an apartment."

"If you want, I can start looking for you. It's not like I have anything better to do."

Kara gave me a soft smile as she grabbed my hand. "Are you sure Max won't stay after your arrangement is over?"

"Yeah. I'm positive. I don't know what his plans are and I don't want to know. He has deep-rooted family issues and he has no intentions of settling with me. I can't go through the emotional pain of hoping we have a future. It's not fair to me."

"You're right. Just hang in there, Emma. We'll be back soon and then we'll get your mind off of him."

I gave them each one last hug and waved goodbye as they went through security. I sighed as I hailed a cab back to my apartment. I put on my workout clothes and went down to the gym and jumped on the treadmill. As I was running, I couldn't help but think about last night. The party was okay, but the best part was what took place in Max's bedroom. The hunger he had for me when I told him that maybe I would contact Lucas after we split up was unlike anything I'd ever experienced before. I could tell he was jealous and didn't want to hear of another man. But was he jealous enough to keep me? Could his jealousy overrule his non-commitment issues? Before I knew it, I had been running on the treadmill for over an hour. I was sweaty and desperately needed a shower. I grabbed the towel and wiped my face as I walked back up to my apartment.

I turned on the hot water and let it run for a minute before stepping into the shower. I looked in the mirror and placed my finger on the butterfly pendant Max gave me. The words he spoke haunted me. *"I always want you to dance, Emma. Promise me you'll never stop dancing."* I didn't think too much about it when he said it to me because I was overwhelmed and we were running late for the party. But after settling into bed last night, it was all I heard. I didn't tell Molly or Kara what he said because they'd make a big deal about it. My feeling was that he gave it to me to keep as a memory of him and the times we spent together after he was gone. Just as I was stepping into the shower, my phone rang and it was my mom. I'd call her back after I was finished with my shower. If she only knew what the hell I was involved in, she'd be mortified.

I stepped out of the shower and put on a pair of yoga pants and an oversized t-shirt. It was seven o'clock and I wasn't planning on going anywhere. I hadn't heard from Max all day and I was feeling a bit lonely without Molly and Kara. I heated up a couple slices of leftover pizza, poured a glass of wine, and called my mom.

"Hey, honey. How are you?"

When I heard her voice, tears came to my eyes. I missed her.

"I'm okay, Mom. How are you?"

"I'm good. Is something wrong? You sound down."

The lump in my throat was getting worse because I just wanted to break down to her, but I didn't want her to worry.

"I'm fine. Kara and Molly left today, so I'm just feeling a little down."

"Aw, sweetheart. Haven't you made any new friends yet?"

"Yeah. I have. I'm just a little homesick."

"How are the men in New York City? Have you met anyone special yet?"

"No. I really don't have time for that right now with school."

"You have to have some fun, Emma. When is Macy coming back?"

"Next week, I think."

"That's good. Then you won't be so lonely. Listen, baby girl, I have to go. We're just on our way out to dinner. I love you and I'll talk to you soon."

"Bye, Mom."

As I poured another glass of wine, there was a knock at the door. The only person it could have been was Max and, frankly, I wasn't in the mood to see him. I got up and looked out the peephole and was shocked when I saw Fiona standing there.

"Fiona, hi. What are you doing here?"

"I didn't know where else to go and I can't go home."

She was totally wasted. She stumbled through the door and I grabbed her arm to prevent her from falling over.

"You're drunk."

"Very observant." She smiled.

"Did something happen?"

"Life," she slurred.

I took her over to the couch and made her sit down. I grabbed my wine glass from the table as I saw her reach for it.

"You're so pretty, Emma. I really wish Max would marry you for real. Can I spend the night?"

"Of course you can, but why don't you tell me what happened?"

"Carol and Bradshaw Hamilton. That's what happened. I'm sick of them trying to control my life and pretending we're the perfect little happy family while my father is out fucking women who are barely out of high school. I hate them, Emma. They're such hypocrites."

I wrapped my arms around her and hugged her as she cried.

"I'm going to be sick. Where's the bathroom?"

"Around the corner. First door on your right." I jumped up as she leaped off the couch with her hand over her mouth.

I heard my phone beep and there was a text message from Max.

"Fiona left home and I can't find her anywhere. My parents are worried sick. You haven't by chance heard from her, have you?"

"She's at my place."

"I'm on my way."

"No, Max. I don't think she wants to see anyone."

"She's my sister, Emma."

I sighed and walked into the bathroom. "Max is on his way over."

"You called him?" she cried.

"No. He just texted me and asked me if I heard from you because you left home and your parents are worried about you. Just talk to him. If anyone understands, he does. I promise you don't have to leave with him. You can still stay here."

Not too long after his text message, there was a knock on the door. I opened it and Max walked right in.

"Where is she?"

"In the bathroom, throwing up. She's drunk."

"Fuck!" He started to walk towards the bathroom.

I grabbed his arm and he looked at me in shock. "Don't yell at her. She's hurting right now and needs your support. I mean it, Max."

He shook his head and went into the bathroom. I followed. He bent down and rubbed her back while I ran a washcloth under warm water and then headed to the kitchen to make some coffee. A few moments later, Max led his sister over to the couch and put his arm around her while they talked.

"I told Fiona that she could stay here tonight."

"Thanks, Emma, but I'll bring her home with me."

"But I want to stay with Emma."

I handed her a cup of coffee. "It's fine, Max. Let her stay."

"I'll call my parents and let her know she's safe here with you."

"I'll leave the two of you alone to talk. I'll be in my room."

About an hour later, Max walked into my room and sat down on the edge of the bed.

"Thanks for helping her out and letting her stay here."

"No problem. How is she?"

"Passed out on the couch. I told her that I don't condone her drinking like that at her age and she told me to fuck off." He chuckled.

"We were seventeen once."

He sighed. "We sure were. Did Molly and Kara get off okay?"

"Yep."

"Is that all you can say?" His lips were dangerously close to mine.

"Uh huh." His scent lured me in. As much as I tried to fight it, I couldn't.

Our lips softly touched as he brought his hand up to my cheek. "I can't stop thinking about last night."

"Yep."

He smiled as he brushed his lips against mine and gently took my bottom lip between his teeth. His hand latched onto my breast as our kiss became more passionate.

"I want to bury my cock deep inside you right now."

I struggled for air because that was what he did to me. He somehow had a way of taking my breath away when he was near.

"I want to press my naked body against yours and feel the softness of your skin. All day, I've been thinking about how good it feels when your pussy is wrapped around my cock."

He stood up, kicked off his shoes, and removed his shirt and pants. I lifted my t-shirt over my head and tossed it on the floor as he hooked his thumbs into the sides of my yoga pants and panties and pulled them off. Climbing under the covers, Max joined me in bed and turned on his side, running his hand down my body and latching onto my breast with his mouth as his fingers dipped inside me. I took in a sharp breath while my hands ran through his hair. I threw my head back as his tongue slid up the flesh of my neck and his fingers manipulated my insides, hitting all the right spots that geared my body up for the ultimate orgasm. My breathing was shallow and my body was on fire. He placed his thumb on my clit and mastered the small circular motion that drove me insane.

"God, I can't wait to be inside of you and feel the warmth of your pussy. Come for me, baby. I won't stop until you come."

I moaned softly and pressed my lips against his as my body seized with the fiery orgasm that took over my entire body, making my toes curl.

"I love it when you come so fierce like that. You have no idea how much it turns me on." He removed his fingers and flipped me over, spreading my legs as he thrust in and out of me while grabbing my ass and squeezing with such a grip that I was about to have another orgasm. His hands grasped my hips and pulled me up so I was on my hands and knees, taking me with long, deep strokes. He groaned as one hand reached around and firmly took hold of my breast, tugging at my hardened nipple, enhancing the sexual pleasure and sending me overboard as the wave was at its peak. I let out a low moan while saying his name as my legs tightened. His movements slowed as he pushed in deeper and moaned as he released himself inside of me. Once he finished, he brought his lips to my back and softly planted small, erotic kisses up and down it. I lowered my head in exhaustion as he pulled out of me and rolled on his back, trying to catch his breath.

"Come here." He held out his arm, motioning for me to snuggle against his warm and muscular chest.

I lay there, wrapped in his arms, thinking about how soon this would all be over; the feeling of security and the feeling of being wanted and needed.

"Will you stay the night?" I asked.

"I really can't, Emma. I have to be up and out early for a meeting tomorrow." He kissed the side of my head, as if that would make me feel better.

I wiggled out of this grip and climbed out of bed.

"Where are you going?"

"I'm going to take a shower. You can let yourself out." I walked in the bathroom and locked the door from behind. Having sex with him was getting to be too much and, being a woman, my emotions were taking over. I turned on the shower so I couldn't hear if he talked to me. Once I finished, I stepped out, wrapped a towel around me, opened the bathroom door, and he was gone. The only thing I saw were the rumpled sheets from where I just had the most incredible sex with a man that I was falling in love with. A man that couldn't love me in return.

Chapter 16

Over the next week, I kept myself busy between school, projects, and apartment hunting for Kara and Molly. Max hadn't bothered to call or text me all week and I didn't really care. As I was on my home from the library, I received a phone call from Macy.

"Oh my God, Macy. How are you?"

"I'm good. Where are you? I'm home!"

Excitement ran through me as the cab pulled up in front of the apartment building. "I'm on my way up right now! I can't wait to see you."

"Hurry and get up here."

As soon as I stepped off the elevator, Macy was standing in the doorway with the door open. We both squealed as I threw down my bag and hugged her.

"Welcome home. It's so good to see you!"

"It's good to see you too. Now get in here and tell me what's been going on. I stopped on the way home and picked us up some grilled chicken salads and a bottle of wine. I hope you're hungry."

"I'm starving," I replied.

Macy looked really good. She hadn't changed a bit since I saw her last year back in Miami. Her blonde hair was still long and straight and she was as skinny as ever. We met three years ago when her mom started working at the diner with my mom. I was in there having lunch one day and she walked in and we got to talking and hit it off right away. She moved to New York a few months later to pursue her modeling career and we kept in touch almost every day. Our friendship grew and when I told her my plans to attend Parsons, she told me to come and stay at her place for as long as I wanted to.

"So, tell me what's been going on in your life since I've been away."

"Ugh. So much has happened you're not even going to believe it. We have a mutual friend here in New York."

"Really?" She smiled. "Who?"

"Max Hamilton."

"How do you know Max? He tried hitting on me a few times when I had parties here."

"I believe it. Anyway, I'm engaged to him."

I felt bad for just blurting it out because she spit out her wine all over the table. Her eyes widened as she looked at me.

"WHAT?! How? Max Hamilton doesn't settle. He's one of New York's most eligible playboys. He's right up there with Collin Black."

"Who?" I asked.

"Another fucking hottie. But, anyway, how the hell did you snag Max Hamilton?"

I explained to her the entire story and I knew she wouldn't tell anyone. We had shared many secrets over the last three years and I knew things about her that would have made people's head spin.

"I'm speechless, Emma. I don't know what to say. But I do understand where both of you are coming from and I completely understand why you agreed to it. I'm just really sorry that Parsons did that to you."

"Me too. My life would be completely different if they hadn't taken back that loan."

"Are you falling for him?" she asked.

I looked down.

"Aw, sweetie. You are." She reached across the table and grabbed my hand. "There's something I need to tell you. The modeling agency is moving me to Paris."

"Oh my God! That's wonderful. I'd love to live in Paris."

"Thanks. I'm pretty excited about it. They want me to leave next week and they're selling the apartment, so I'm afraid you'll have to move."

Panic settled in. Where was I going to go? I couldn't afford an apartment on my own. I didn't have a job yet. *Shit.*

"No problem. I've been looking at apartments for Kara and Molly anyway and I've seen a few that I liked. I'm so happy for you, but it sucks because you just got home and now you're moving away in a week."

"I know, sweetie. I'm sorry."

I stood up and gave her a hug. "Don't be sorry. This is an amazing opportunity for you."

"Maybe you can stay with Max." She smiled.

"Umm. No. That wouldn't work out too well." I laughed.

We cleaned up, talked some more, and then headed off to bed. She'd had a long flight and was jet lagged, and I needed to call Molly and Kara and figure out what to do.

****

The next day after class let out, I resumed my apartment hunt. I heard my phone ringing and I pulled it from my purse to see that Max was calling. I sighed.

"Hello."

"Hey. What are you doing?"

"Apartment hunting."

"Why?"

"One, for Kara and Molly, and two, because I have to move."

"What do you mean? Wait. Explain to me over dinner. I'll be by to pick you up at six o'clock."

"No. I don't want to go to dinner."

"Sorry, Emma. You're breaking up. I can't hear you. Bad connection. See you at six." *Click.*

Damn him! The last thing I needed today was to see him. He hadn't called all week and now he decided he wanted to see me. Fuck him. When I got home, Macy had just walked through the door.

"Hey. How was school?"

"It was okay. I have to hurry and change. Max is coming to pick me up for dinner."

"Oh. It'll be nice to see him again. I think." She laughed.

I went to my bedroom and changed my clothes. As I was freshening up my makeup and running the brush through my hair, I heard a knock at the door. Macy answered it.

"Well, if it isn't Mr. Hamilton. Do come in," I heard Macy say.

"Emma didn't tell me that you had returned."

"Maybe because you hadn't bothered to call me all week." I glared at his sexiness as I walked past him.

"I was out of town on business. Anyway, it's good to see you again, Macy. Now, what's this about you having to move?" he asked.

"The magazine I'm going to be doing exclusives with is in Paris. I'm moving next week, and my agency is selling the apartment. I feel really bad, but there's nothing I can do."

"I told you last night that it's fine. I'll find something. In fact, I saw a couple of apartments today I'm going to inquire about."

I didn't want to tell her or Max that I couldn't afford it. If I had to, I'd use the money Max gave me for the next semester's tuition and get a job right away. I was sure I'd have no problem finding a waitressing job at one of the upscale restaurants. Kara and Molly told me to move in with them, but trying to find a three-bedroom apartment at a reasonable price we all could afford was extremely difficult. Plus, the apartments were so small and the three of us would be too cramped.

"I can help you find a place, Emma," Max said as he gave me a small smile.

"No. It's fine. You've done enough and I can find one on my own. Now, let's go to dinner. I need to get back. I have homework to do before tomorrow."

I grabbed my purse, kissed Macy on the cheek, and told her I'd see her later. Max placed his hand on the small of my back, which sent shivers throughout my body. I would never get over his touch and how it made me feel. I climbed in the Rolls Royce and said hello to Darren. He gave me a smile and a wink. It had been a while since I'd seen him. He dropped us off at the curb of a restaurant called Eleven Madison Park, where the menu was $225 a person.

"Don't you think this is a bit expensive?"

"No. Not at all. They have some of the best food here. Don't worry about the price."

"So where did you go on business this week?" I asked as I sipped my mojito.

"California. I needed to meet with Ian Braxton regarding some property I'm interested in that he owns in Chicago."

"Chicago?"

"Yeah. I'm looking at a building for my company."

He was confusing me. "What do you mean *your* company? What about your father's company?"

"What about it? I'm branching out on my own as soon as my trust fund comes through. I'm building a software company. This is between you and me. Nobody knows about this."

"And what is your father going to say about this?"

"It's none of my father's business. Maybe if he spent more time being a father, I wouldn't feel the need to get out from under him. We got in an argument right before I left for California. I confronted him about his affairs and how it was affecting me and Fiona. I told him he was a hypocrite and the perfect Hamilton family was nothing but a joke. He told me to mind my own business and continue to act like the prodigal son. I swear I can't stand that man. I want nothing to do with Hamilton Reality, Hamilton Development Group, or Hamilton Investments. I'm starting my own company and I'm building my own success out from underneath my father."

As I sat there and listened to his rant, which was very uncontrolled for even Max, I felt sorry for him.

"Have you thought of talking to your mom?"

He laughed. "There's no talking to her. He has full control over her. She would never think about stepping out of line and defying Mr. Bradshaw Hamilton. She agrees with everything he says. She always has."

"Even if she found out about his affairs?"

"My mother appears to be a strong woman, but in reality, she's very weak. I hate him, Emma. I really do."

I reached across the table and took hold of his hand. "I'm sorry, Max."

"It's funny because people think that when you have money and a high-powered established name, all is glorious in the world. It's so far from the truth. I just want my trust fund and to get out of his shadow. The day I turn twenty-six is the day that I throw a wrench in all their perfect plans."

"Why Chicago? Why not stay in New York?"

"Because I want as far away from my parents as possible."

The sadness in his eyes consumed me. I knew he had problems with his father, but I never knew it was to this extent. I guessed that after we broke up, he'd be moving to Chicago and I'd never see him again. He had no intentions of staying in New York.

After we ate, he took me back to my apartment and walked me to the door. He placed his hand on my cheek and softly kissed my lips. "Thank you again for doing this for me."

"You're welcome." I smiled softly.

"I'll be in touch soon." He kissed my forehead and turned and walked away.

A feeling of comfort washed over me as I watched him walk down the hall.

"Max!" I yelled.

He stopped and turned around. I threw my purse down and ran to him, wrapping my arms around his neck and giving him the most passionate kiss possible.

"Promise me you'll always dance."

"Only if you will." He smiled.

Chapter 17

All of Macy's boxes were packed and sitting in the hallway for the company to come pick up and ship off to Paris.

"You sure you have everything?" I asked as I gave her a pout.

"Yep. I sure do. Here's my key to the apartment."

"Are you sure I can stay an extra couple of weeks?"

"Yeah. My agency said the new buyer isn't in any hurry to move in and that he understands your situation."

I gave her a long hug as tears filled my eyes. "Good luck in Paris and I'll be seeing you in all the magazines."

"I'll let you know when I get there and we'll skype just like we used to. Keep me posted on things with Max."

"I will. I love you, Macy. Have a safe trip."

"Love you too, girl. I'll talk to you soon."

Just as she was walking out the door, Max, whom I hadn't seen in over a week, walked in.

"Hey, Macy. Have a good trip and be safe in Paris."

"Thanks, Max. Good luck with everything."

Max shut the door and looked at me before wrapping his arms around me and pulling me into a warm embrace. "You okay?"

"Yeah. I'm just a little sad she's gone. We barely got to spend any time together."

"I know. I'm sorry. How about we order in and then watch a movie? Maybe have a little sex to take your mind off things."

I lifted my head. "Did you just really say that?"

He chuckled. "Yeah, I did. Sorry."

I smacked him on the chest and asked him what he wanted for dinner. "By the way, where were you all week?"

"Working. Between my dad's company and trying to get things settled with my new company, it's been crazy."

I understood and I was already getting used to the fact that he wasn't around much. It was probably for the best anyway, since we only had two weeks left of our engagement. Max would turn twenty-six next week and we would break up a week later.

"I bought you something." He smiled as he pulled a tissue-wrapped item out of his pocket.

"For what?"

"Open it."

I slowly unwrapped the tissue paper and inside was a beautiful sterling silver crystal butterfly key ring. I held it up and smiled.

"It's beautiful, Max. You shouldn't have. Thank you."

"You're welcome. It's for your new apartment key."

"Thank you. As soon as I get it, I'll put it right on." I reached up and kissed his lips.

"You already have your new apartment key."

"What do you mean? I haven't found an apartment yet."

"Yes, you have. This one."

"Huh?" I asked in confusion.

He placed his hands on my hips. "You're staying right here. I bought the apartment for you from Macy's modeling agency. You get to live here rent free for as long as you need to. Now you don't have to worry about being able to afford rent and moving."

Tears filled my eyes as I stared up at him. "No, Max. I can't let you do that."

"It's already done. Emma, I don't want to have to worry about you and where you're living when we're no longer together. This is your apartment. You should be happy."

"I am happy. Very happy, but you've done enough for me already. This is just too much." A tear fell down my face.

"It's not too much." He wiped away the tear from my cheek and then gently brushed his lips against mine. "I want to make sweet love to you," his soft voice spoke.

"Please do." I smiled.

He picked me up and carried me into the bedroom, where we spent the next hour making love.

****

Max and I saw each other a couple of times over the next week. We had dinner with his parents, which was awkward because of the tension between Max and his dad, and then we attended the opening of a new restaurant that one of Max's friends owned. I had found an apartment for Kara and Molly and sent them videos to get their thoughts. They loved it and the best part was that it was only about ten minutes from my apartment. I couldn't wait for them to fly in tomorrow and I even decided to take the day off from school to help them move in. I moved into the master bedroom in my place and bought a new comforter and sheets for the bed. Max hung a few pictures for me and with the placement of a few candles, my bedroom was complete.

The next morning, I picked up Kara and Molly at the airport.

"I can't believe the two of you are here for good!" I exclaimed as the three of us hugged.

"We can't believe it either. I'm so excited to see the apartment!" Molly smiled.

"When are the movers coming with all your things?"

"They said they'll be here around noon."

Their apartment was located on the third floor with a private balcony. It had an oversized living room, hardwood floors throughout, and a decent-sized kitchen with a wraparound counter top.

"This is amazing!" Kara said excitedly as we walked through the apartment. "Look at the closet space."

"You did good, Emma." Molly smiled as she hooked her arm around me.

"Thanks. I must say it's a nice place and the rent is pretty decent for two people to split."

Just as they were unpacking their suitcases, there was a knock on the door.

"I'll get it," I yelled from the kitchen.

When I opened the door, there were two men wearing blue jumpsuits standing there.

"We have a TV delivery."

"Kara, Molly, your TV is here."

They emerged from their bedrooms and looked at the guys in blue suits.

"We didn't order a TV. You must have the wrong apartment."

The heavyset man looked at the invoice and then at the apartment number on the door. "Nope. This is the right apartment. "We'll go grab it off the truck and you need to tell us which wall you want it mounted on."

"What the fuck is going on?" Kara asked.

A few moments later, the two men carried in the seventy-inch LED HD TV. "Where do you want it?"

There was only one wall in the living room that it would fit on, opposite the door wall.

"This wall right here, please," Molly spoke.

"Here's a card that came with the TV for a Kara and Molly."

Kara took it from the deliveryman and opened the envelope.

Happy housewarming and welcome to New York.

You're going to love it!

Love, Max

"Wow. It's from Max."

"What? Let me see that." I took the card from her and couldn't believe it.

"What a great guy." Molly smiled.

I gave her a small smile and went back to the kitchen.

We spent the day getting all their stuff organized, and once the movers brought their furniture, we left and went shopping for some kitchen and bath essentials. By time I got back to my apartment, it was already eleven o'clock and I was exhausted. I changed into my pajamas, took off my makeup, and as I went to the kitchen to grab a bottle of water from the fridge, my phone beeped with a text message from Max.

"Are you up?"

"Yeah, just about to go to bed. I'm exhausted."

"Open your door."

I looked at his last message in confusion, set my phone down, and opened the door.

"Hi." He smiled.

"What are you doing here?"

"I was hoping to spend the night with you. You look tired." He walked in and wrapped his arms around me.

"I am. It was a long day and, yes, I would like you to spend the night."

The tone in his voice seemed sad and I found it odd that he would drop by unannounced at eleven o'clock at night. I could tell something was bothering him, but I was too afraid to ask. We walked into the bedroom and I took off my nightshirt and climbed under the covers while he took off his shirt and pants. He climbed in next to me and wrapped his arms around me, pulling me into him.

"I just want to hold you and fall asleep. No sex tonight if that's okay with you."

"It's fine, Max. Good night." I lifted my head and kissed him on the lips. He smiled as he pushed a strand of my hair away from my face.

"Good night, Emma."

I laid my head on his chest and closed my eyes as he reached over and turned off the light. *What was going on with him?*

Chapter 18

I opened my eyes and quickly jumped out of bed, running to the bathroom and hovering over the toilet.

"Are you okay?" Max asked with concern.

"I don't think so." I began vomiting.

Max entered the bathroom and pulled back my hair, rubbing my back as I vomited a few more times.

"Do you have the flu?" He handed me a tissue.

"It's possible. A few students at school had just had it, so I know it's going around."

"You better go back to bed and get some rest."

"I can't. I have that huge project to turn in today. I have to go to classes."

"But if you're sick, you can't."

I stood up and splashed some cold water on my face. "I'll be fine. I have no choice."

"We have about an hour before we need to be up and ready, so let's go back to bed for a bit."

He helped me into bed and climbed in next to me. I snuggled up against him and closed my eyes. Before I knew it, he was waking me up.

"Emma, you have to get up or you'll be late. Are you okay?"

When I opened my eyes, Max was standing over me, fully dressed and ready to leave.

"Yeah. I'll be fine." I climbed out of bed. I didn't have the energy to shower, so I just threw my hair up in a ponytail, and pulled on a pair of black leggings and an oversized sweater. Fall had settled in New York and it was getting chillier by the day. I wasn't used to November weather anywhere but Miami. Max gave me a kiss and said goodbye.

"I'll call you later to see how you're doing. Try to take it easy today and come right home after school."

"I will. Have a good day at work."

I pulled the orange juice out of the fridge and poured myself a glass. My stomach still had that sick feeling, but it wasn't anything I couldn't handle. No matter how I felt later, I needed to stop by the jewelers and pick up Max's birthday gift. His birthday was in a couple of days and we were going out to dinner with his parents and Fiona. As the day went on, I could barely keep my eyes open in class. Hannah wasn't in class today because she was sick with the flu. When my last class got out, I saw Darren waiting at the curb. He smiled.

"How are you feeling, Emma? Max told me you were sick this morning."

"I'm not doing too well, Darren. What are you doing here?"

"Max sent me to pick you up and make sure you go straight home."

I sighed. "That was nice of him, but I need you to take me to the jewelers first. I have to pick up his birthday present. It'll only take a minute."

"Of course." He opened the door for me and I slid in the back seat.

As soon as Darren dropped me off at my apartment, I set down my purse and climbed into bed. I awoke to the ringing sound of my phone.

"Hello."

"Were you sleeping?" Max asked.

"Yeah. What time is it?"

"Seven o'clock. I was going to bring you over some chicken soup. Are you up for some?"

"That sounds good. Thank you."

"I'll see you in a bit."

I couldn't believe that I had slept for three hours. It was a good thing I didn't have classes tomorrow because I just wanted to stay home and rest.

"I've unlocked the door. I'm going to take a quick shower. Let yourself in."

Stripping out of my clothes, I stepped into the shower and stood under the hot water, hoping that it would wake me up. Once I was finished, I stepped out and heard Max talking from the living room. He must have been on the phone. After drying off and slipping into my pajamas, I followed the aroma of chicken soup to the kitchen.

"Hey. How are you feeling?" he asked as he put his phone in his pocket.

"Like crap." I smiled.

"You may feel like crap, but you don't look like it."

I gave him a small smile as he took down a bowl from the cabinet and filled it with soup. I grabbed a bottle of water from the fridge and sat down at the table.

"Thanks for bringing this over. If you wouldn't have called me, I don't think I would have gotten up. Hannah wasn't in school today. Apparently, she's sick with the flu as well."

"Ah, it must be going around. I'm sure you'll feel better in the morning after you get a good night's sleep."

"You're a good friend, Hamilton." I smiled as I held up my spoon.

"So are you."

****

Max didn't spend the night. He was flying out to Chicago first thing in the morning to meet some lawyers about his software company and said that he'd be back tonight. My stomach was feeling queasy as I got out of bed and headed to the bathroom. I couldn't believe I'd slept until ten o'clock. As I started to brush my teeth, I could feel the vomit rise up in my throat. I threw my tooth brush down and leaned over the toilet. As I grabbed a tissue and wiped my mouth, I heard my phone from the bedroom ring.

"Hi, Mom," I answered as I climbed back into bed.

"Hi, Emma. What's wrong? Did I wake you?"

"No. I was up. I have the flu."

"Oh no. When did that start?"

"Yesterday."

"Make sure you drink plenty of fluids. You don't want to get dehydrated."

"I know, Mom. Was there a reason why you called?"

"No. Nothing in particular. I just wanted to catch up and see how you were doing. Give me a call when you're feeling better."

"Okay, Mom. I'll talk to you soon."

The overwhelming guilt that I hadn't told her what was going on was still with me and I felt like shit for keeping it from her. But if I had told her, she'd worry, and that was the last thing I wanted. As I laid my head on the pillow, a text message from Max came through.

"Good morning. How are you feeling today?"

"A little better."

"Good to hear. Make sure you rest all day. You have to be better for my birthday tomorrow."

"Don't worry. I will be. Have a good day in Chicago."

"I will. I'll be over later tonight when I get back and hopefully you'll feel better for some great sex." He sent me the winky face.

"Looking forward to it."

I didn't want to tell him that I was still sick because I didn't want him to worry. As I lay on the couch and binge-watched *Veronica Mars*, I kept thinking about Max and how, in a week, my life would completely change.

****

His hand cupped my breast as the warmth of his tongue slid up my throat. I wrapped my legs around his waist as he thrust inside me, moving slowly and passionately. Our mouths met with delight and my fingers played in his hair as he moved in and out of me fluently, bringing me to my second orgasm of the night. His sexy moans deepened as he exploded inside of me.

"I hope that made you feel better." He smiled as he placed his hand on my forehead.

"It did."

He kissed my lips before rolling off of me and headed to the bathroom.

"Someone has a big birthday coming up in a couple of hours."

He emerged from the bathroom with a smile on his face but still a hint of sadness in his eyes. He climbed into bed and wrapped his arms around me.

"I can't think of a better way to wake up on my birthday than with your perfect naked body wrapped around mine."

I gave his chest tiny kisses as I placed my hand down below, feeling his cock over the cotton of his underwear.

"I think this big guy may get his own present in the morning." I felt it twinge and I smiled.

"I'm going to make sure you keep that promise." He kissed my head and turned off the light.

The next morning, I made good on my promise and gave him an amazing birthday present.

"Happy birthday, big boy." I smiled as I finished and kissed his lips.

"Damn. It sure is a happy birthday. Thank you." He cupped his hand around the back of my neck and pulled me into a passionate kiss. "I guess you're feeling better."

"I am and I have something for you." I reached in the drawer in the nightstand and pulled out the small gift bag. "Happy birthday, Max."

He sat up against the headboard and took the box from the bag. "You didn't have to get me anything."

"I wanted to. Now open it."

He removed the lid and pulled out the stainless steel and black onyx pendant with his name engraved on a black leather rope.

"Emma, this is amazing."

"Do you like it? I thought you could wear it when you dress a little more casually."

"I love it."

"Turn it over." I smiled.

He ran his finger over the small phoenix that I had engraved. "The phoenix, much like the butterfly, symbolizes transformation and rebirth. I thought it was appropriate since you're embarking on a new adventure and renewing yourself out from under your father's shadow."

"I'm speechless. No one has ever given me something like this before. I don't know what to say."

"You don't have to say anything. It's a gift from me to you."

"Thank you. I'll wear it every day."

"I have to get ready for school and you have to get ready for the office." I smiled.

"I'm going to call Darren to come get me and take me home real quick. I left some papers there that I need." He kissed me.

I got up from the bed and went into the bathroom to brush my teeth. The feeling of nausea returned the minute I put the toothbrush in my mouth. I quickly removed it and placed my hands on the counter, waiting for it to pass.

"Darren's here and I'm heading out. I'll be by to pick you up around five thirty," he said through the door.

"Okay. Have a great day and I'll see you later. Happy birthday, Max!"

"Thanks, babe. I'll call you later."

He couldn't get out fast enough for me as I leaned over the toilet and started vomiting. *Shit*. What was going on? I didn't have time for this. I got ready and headed out the door to school. When I arrived and sat down in my seat, Hannah came strolling in.

"Hey, how are you feeling?" I asked her.

"A little better. That flu really kicked my ass."

"Tell me about it. I'm still not feeling well and I have that dinner tonight with Max and his family. It's his birthday."

"Oh yeah, that's right. It's almost over. How are you feeling about that?"

"I'm okay," I totally lied. "It's hard to believe that the last three months went by so fast."

"I know. We're almost done with this semester."

I sighed. "As soon as the semester ends, I have to find a job. My money is running out."

"The bookstore on campus is hiring. I don't know how much they pay, but it's worth a shot." She smiled.

"Maybe I'll check it out. Thanks, Hannah."

"Hey, I'm not feeling so well," Austin said as he leaned in between us. "I think I need to leave."

Hannah and I looked at him. He was as white as a ghost. "You better get home before you start puking all over us."

"I'll talk to you girls later." He grabbed his things and literally ran out of the classroom.

We both laughed. "Poor Austin."

Chapter 19

After dinner, we went back to Max's parents' house for cake and ice cream. Dinner was awkward because all Carol wanted to talk about was the wedding and all the things she thought I should do. I helped Carol put twenty-six candles on the large and beautifully decorated cake that she had made for Max. We lit each one and carried it into the dining room where Max, Fiona, and Bradshaw were waiting for us.

"Happy birthday to you. Happy birthday to you. Happy birthday, dear Max. Happy birthday to you," we sang as we walked in and set the cake down in front of him.

I leaned over and whispered in his ear, "Make a wish."

He blew out the candles and we all clapped. Bradshaw stood up and left the room. A few moments later, he walked in and handed Max an envelope.

"Happy birthday, son. I've signed off on your trust fund and now it's all yours. I have no doubt that you'll be responsible with it."

"Thanks, Dad. Thanks, Mom."

"We are so happy for you and Emma, darling. Now let's set a date so we can get working on this wedding."

"Oh, Max and I have already set a date. We were waiting to tell you." Max looked at me with surprise as I grabbed his hand. "We are getting married on September 10, 2016."

"Oh. A September wedding. How perfect!" Carol smiled.

"Congratulations, you two." Bradshaw winked at Max.

"That's less than a year. We better start planning."

Max put up his hand. "Whoa, Mom. We just set the date. Give us some time."

After finishing cake and ice cream, Max took me upstairs to his bedroom.

"Are you okay? You look exhausted."

"I'm really tired. It's been a long day and I don't think I'm fully recovered yet."

"Then let's get you home." His thumb grazed over my cheek. "Nice touch about the wedding date."

"Thanks. Your mom was getting on my nerves." I laughed.

****

"So how did it go last night at dinner?" Kara asked as she and Molly sat across from me in the restaurant.

"I told them we set a date. September 10, 2016. I couldn't stand Carol's whining anymore."

"When are you breaking it off?" Molly frowned.

"Next Friday night. We're going to his parents' house for dinner." I picked at my salad.

"What's wrong? Are you still sick?" Kara asked. "You're barely eating."

"Yeah. This flu is killing me."

"Maybe it's not the flu. Maybe you're making yourself sick over what's to come. It happens, you know."

"I don't know. I don't want to end things with Max. I know we were never a real couple, but I like being with him."

"Maybe once all is said and done, he'll change his mind and not want to let you go."

"I doubt it. I almost told him the other day that I loved him. I had to catch myself and then I started to panic. What if I would have said it?"

"It's a good thing you didn't because there's no telling how he might have reacted."

The two of them finished dinner and I had mine wrapped up to go. Maybe tomorrow I'd finish it.

****

I'd spent the week going to school and then coming home and taking long naps. I hadn't seen Max since his birthday but we talked a few times. We had put our plan in motion for tonight and I was a nervous wreck. Maybe the girls were right. Maybe I was making myself sick over this whole thing and depression seemed to be settling in. But I had a tiny piece of hope that I clung to that Max would tell me that he loved me and he'd call this whole break-up thing off.

"You ready?" he asked as he took my hand.

"As ready as I'll ever be." My stomach was twisted in the tightest knot possible.

We sat down for dinner with Carol and Bradshaw and the game began as I looked at Max.

"I don't understand why you couldn't have called today. You told me you would, but as usual, you can never keep your word."

"Not now, Emma. I already explained to you how busy I was."

His parents looked uncomfortable as they kept their heads down while they ate.

"So is this how it's going to be, Max? Work before me?"

"Emma, I'm not discussing this now," he spoke through gritted teeth.

"That's your problem. You never want to discuss anything. Half the time, I feel shut out."

I threw my napkin down on the table and got up and walked away. Walking outside to the back patio like we planned, he followed.

"Throw your hands around. Yell. Press your finger into my chest in case they're watching."

I did just that. We yelled back and forth and put on a good show for his parents. I took the ring off, placed it in his hand, and stormed through the patio door.

"It's over, Max. I just can't take it anymore. I can't be with a man who puts his work before me. I should be the number one priority in your life. Me, Max. Your fiancée. The girl you supposedly love."

"Emma, please don't do this. I'll change. I promise."

"You've already shown me that you can't keep your promises and I refuse to live my life with someone like that. I can't. I just can't!"

I stormed out the front door and climbed into the Rolls Royce, where Darren was waiting for me. Tears started to stream down my face because the reality of what happened and what was to come hit me. I wanted to throw up.

"I'm sorry, Emma," Darren spoke as he handed me a tissue.

"It's okay. We knew this fucking day was coming and I thought I was prepared. But the truth is I love him, Darren."

"I know you do and I'm sorry."

My phone beeped with a text message from Max.

"My parents are highly upset. Try to get some sleep and I'll come by in the morning."

I couldn't bring myself to answer him back. I continued to shake as Darren helped me from the car.

"I have faith that things will work out, Emma."

"I doubt it, Darren. Thanks for the ride."

"Have a good night."

I entered my apartment and headed straight to the bedroom. After changing into my pajamas, I climbed into bed and laid my head down as the uncontrollable tears fell.

****

I could barely open my swollen eyes as I had to make my way to the bathroom to throw up. I tossed and turned all night from the nightmares I had. I splashed my face with cold water and grabbed my phone to see if Max had messaged me. He hadn't. It was nine o'clock and I didn't know what time he was coming over. I needed to talk to him and tell him that I was in love with him. I couldn't just let him walk away from this not knowing. It was a risk, but I was willing to take it. As I walked to the kitchen to make some coffee, I stopped when I saw a white envelope lying in front of the door, almost as if someone had slipped it under. I walked over, picked it up, and ran my finger across my name, which was written on it. I nervously opened it and took out the white stationery that was folded inside.

My dearest Emma,

I'm writing you this letter because I can't bear to say goodbye to you in person. Last night was one of the toughest nights of my life. Although we had this planned for the past three months, it still felt incredibly real. I'll always cherish and never forget the time we spent together and getting to know one *another. You are an incredible and loving person and you deserve only the best. And believe me, I wish I was the best, but I'm not. Not only are you the most beautiful woman that I've ever laid eyes on, you're incredibly talented and smart. There's something about you that makes people feel good when they're around you. Even if I had the shittiest day, just knowing that I was going to see you made it all better. Call me a coward for hiding behind these words because that's exactly what I am. I know I've hurt you and I'm sorry and I hope one day you can forgive me. It's time for me to step out of the shadow of my father and discover the man who I truly am. I've always dreamed of starting my own company away from my father's and now, thanks to you, I can do just that. I know this is probably as hard for you to read as it is for me to write. I'm a flawed man, Emma, and you deserve someone who's flawless. Because that's exactly what you are. Promise me you'll never stop dancing and take full advantage of what life has to offer you. I've opened a bank account in your name in the sum of $250,000. I don't want you to worry about having to find a job and living expenses. I've also set up an account at Parsons in your name with the rest of the tuition money until you graduate. Go to school and live your dream. You deserve it. Good-bye, my sweetest Emma. Love always, Max.*

I dropped the letter and fell to my knees, sobbing and shaking, trying to get hold of my emotions. The hope I had was gone and I had nothing left. I set myself up for agreeing to this proposed deal and I knew the more we became involved, the harder it would be to let go. I got up from the floor and lay down on the couch, where I spent the rest of the day. Kara and Molly came over after they finished working at the salon, and as soon as they walked in, they saw the letter on the floor. Molly bent down and picked it up while Kara came over and wrapped her arms around me and I continued to cry on her shoulder.

Chapter 20

A week had passed and I wasn't any better. Hannah and Austin dropped by a couple of times to check up on me because I hadn't been in school. I couldn't bring myself to leave the apartment. All I did was sleep. On a Thursday night, there was a knock at the door. Kara was supposed to come over, so I thought it was her. To my surprise, when I opened the door, I saw Bradshaw standing there.

"We need to talk." He stormed past me in anger.

"I'm really not up to—"

"I don't give a fuck what you're not up to!" he yelled. "Was this whole engagement a sham? Did you help Max out so he could collect his trust fund and leave?"

"Talk to your son. Now I want you to leave."

I wasn't about to talk to him about this.

"I'm not going anywhere until you tell me everything!" He walked up to me and grabbed my arms, gripping them tight. "Do you have any idea what you've done? You filthy little whore!"

Suddenly, and out of nowhere, a strength rose inside of me as I got out of his grip.

"Don't you ever fucking touch me again or I swear to you that I will call the police. Imagine what the headlines would say. Imagine what Carol and Fiona would say. You disgusting pig! How dare you fucking blame me for Max's behavior. It was because of YOU that he did what he did. Always walking in your shadow, expected to be the perfect son. Your dirty affairs with all your whores you've had over the years and then threatening your child if he told his mother! What kind of father are you? How do you feel that you've scarred your son from the age of thirteen when he saw you in Hawaii fucking another woman who wasn't his mother?"

The look on his face was complete shock. The door opened and Kara walked in.

"What the fuck is going on in here? I can hear you all the way down the hall."

"Mr. Hamilton was just leaving," I spewed.

He turned and walked out the door without saying a word, shutting it behind him. I stood there, trying to calm down when, suddenly, I felt an intense cramping in my stomach. I doubled over in pain and Kara ran to me.

"Emma, what's wrong?"

"I don't know. I having horrible cramps."

She lightly took hold of my arm and led me to the couch. "I was talking to a girl at the salon about how you can't shake this flu and she said that you could be having appendicitis. That would explain your vomiting and nauseous feeling."

"Oh God, Kara. It hurts."

"That's it. I'm taking you to the hospital."

****

I lay in the hospital bed with Kara by my side when Molly entered the room.

"Hey. How are you feeling?"

"Not so good," I pouted.

"Any news yet?" she asked with concern.

"No. Not yet. I've only seen the nurse."

A few moments later, a woman wearing a white coat walked into my room. "Hi, Emma. I'm Dr. Edmonds and I'm going to do an abdominal ultrasound on you. We sent your blood work to the lab, but they're very backed up, so this ultrasound will let me see what's going on and whether or not you need to be taken into surgery right away. Can you lift up your gown to right below your breasts, please?"

I did as she asked and she turned off the lights and placed the wand on my abdomen. She moved it back and forth across me and then suddenly stopped.

"May I ask that your friends step out of the room, please?"

"It's okay, Dr. Edmonds. They're my best friends. They can stay. Is something wrong?"

She turned her head and looked at me with a smile. "You're pregnant."

I gulped and Kara's and Molly's eyes widened as they looked at me.

"I'm sorry, but you're mistaken. I can't be pregnant. I'm on the pill."

"See this right here?" She pointed to the screen. "That's the embryo and there's the heartbeat."

I was in shock as I stared at the screen. I went numb.

"When was your last period?" she asked.

"I don't know. I can't remember. I've been so busy over the past few months that I didn't really pay attention."

"The pill is only 99% effective if you take it correctly. If you skip a day or two, then double up, it can throw everything off and your chances of getting pregnant increase."

SHIT! SHIT! SHIT!

"Have you been under a great deal of stress lately?"

"Yes."

She smiled as she placed her hand on mine. "It's important that you cut the stress out of your life immediately. From what I can tell, everything looks fine and I don't see any problems. I am going to do a vaginal check, though, just to make sure you aren't spotting. So I'll need your friends to step out for a moment."

Kara and Molly walked out of the room and I placed my feet in the stirrups. Dr. Edmonds did the exam and said everything looked fine.

"I'm going to go check and see if your blood work is ready yet. Once I confirm everything there, then you can leave."

"How far along am I?"

"You're about six weeks. Do you have an OB/GYN?"

"No. I just moved to New York about three months ago."

"I'll give you the card of a wonderful obstetrician. I want you to call him and make an appointment within the week. When you do, have his office call the hospital and we'll send over your medical file. Is the dad in the picture?" she asked.

I shook my head.

"Well, you have options. I want you to go home, get off your feet for the rest of the weekend, and relax. Your baby was telling you to slow down. I'll go tell your friends they can come back in. You can get dressed."

Kara and Molly walked back into the room and grabbed my hands.

"You're going to have a baby." Molly smiled.

Kara didn't say a word. She just gave me a sympathetic look. The three of us took a cab back to my apartment. I changed into my pajamas and climbed into bed.

"When are you going to tell Max?" Kara asked as she sat on the edge of the bed.

"I don't know. I still have to process the fact that I'm pregnant. I can't believe this is happening to me." I started to cry.

"Aw, come here." She wrapped her arms around me. "Everything will work out. You have me and Molly here plus Aubrey will be here in another month."

"How the hell am I going to tell my mom?"

"Your mom will understand, Emma. You're twenty-four years old. It's not like you're sixteen."

"Don't you see? This is history repeating itself. This baby isn't going to have a father just like I didn't."

"You're not going to tell Max?"

"You read the letter, Kara. He left me. He couldn't even say goodbye. He can't even commit to one woman. Do you think he can be a father to a kid? And besides, he's gone. He's not even in New York anymore and I don't think he has any plans on coming back."

Molly walked in the room and handed me a cup of tea. "Did I hear you right that you're not going to tell Max? I don't blame you. I wouldn't tell that piece of shit either. You're going to be fine, Emma. Oh my God, we're going to have a baby!"

"Who are you going to say the father is when people ask?"

"I'll just tell them that it was a one-night stand with some guy I met at a bar. Let people think I'm a whore. Whatever.

Thanks you two for taking care of me, but I'm really tired right now and just want to go to sleep."

"Okay. Text us if you need anything." Kara and Molly hugged me goodbye and left.

As I lay in bed, sipping my tea, I placed my hand on my belly, still in shock there was a baby growing inside of me. I didn't want to be like my mom and raise a kid alone. I had a vision where I was married and we'd find out together that I was pregnant. We'd go through the pregnancy together and the love of my life would be in the delivery room when his child was born. I wasn't supposed to be a single parent. Was I even ready to be a mom? I could barely take care of myself, let alone a baby all on my own.

Chapter 21

Thanksgiving was in a few days and I booked a flight back to Miami. My mom had been bugging me to fly home for Thanksgiving because she desperately missed me. School had ended yesterday for break and I was more than ready to leave the cold weather behind, if only for a few days. I had told Hannah and Austin that I was pregnant and they flipped. When they asked who the father was, I told them with shame that it was a one-night stand.

I packed my suitcase and took a cab to the airport. Kara and Molly were staying back in New York for Thanksgiving because they had to work on Friday. They were going to cook a turkey for the first time and I wished I was there to watch them. But I needed my mom more than ever now and I needed to tell her about the baby. I was so scared.

When I stepped off the plane, I took in a deep breath as I walked through the airport.

"Emma!" I heard my mom yell as she waved both hands in the air.

The minute I saw her, I started to cry.

"Oh, baby. Let me look at you." She smiled as she placed her hands on my face.

"Hi, Mom." I hugged her tight. "I missed you."

"I missed you too, sweetheart. Come on; let's go home."

To keep myself from having a total breakdown in the car, I asked my mom to tell me all about Danny. The way her eyes lit up when she talked about him made me happy. I had never seen her like this before over a guy. For everything she'd been through in life, she deserved to finally be happy.

I took my bag to my room and sat down on the edge of the bed. I was exhausted. Exhaustion had become my best friend these days. As I sat there with my face cupped in my hands, my mom walked into the room.

"Emma, what's wrong with you? You don't seem like yourself. Did something happen in New York that you're not telling me about?"

I could never keep anything from her, even if I wanted to. All she had to do was look at me and she knew when something was wrong. My shoulders began to move up and down as I started to cry in my hands.

"Oh, honey. What is it?" she consoled me as she wrapped her arm around me.

I lifted my head and looked at her. Teary eyed, stuffy nose, and the overwhelming feeling of disappointment she'd have in me.

"I'm pregnant, Mom."

She pursed her lips together and stared at me with her big brown eyes. It wasn't a look of disappointment. It was a look of empathy.

"Emma," she whispered. "Who's the father?"

I laid my head on her shoulder. "It's such a long story, Mom. There's so much you don't know."

"Then tell me." She squeezed my hand.

I told her how I had met Max at the club the night before I left and then about the email from Parsons.

"All I had to do was pretend to be his fiancée and he would pay for my tuition at Parsons. It was only for three months, Mom." I sobbed. "And then I had to go and fall in love with his dumb ass. He couldn't even say goodbye. He slipped a letter under my door. Who does that, Mom?" I continued sobbing. "I really thought he loved me or at least cared enough to stay."

"Sweetheart, it probably hurt him too much to say goodbye in person. Men are cowards and they run. Look at your father."

"I don't know what to do, Mom. I'm so scared."

"And so was I, sweet baby girl. But I never once regretted having you. You are the one good thing that happened in my life and this baby will be for you too, but you have to tell Max about the baby."

"I can't. He's gone and he's starting over. He's making something of himself on his own. If he truly loved me, he never would have left. But he did. I won't destroy his dreams and life with the responsibility of a child."

"Emma, he has a right to know. Let him make his own decision."

"He made his decision the day he slipped that letter under my door and walked out of my life. I obviously didn't mean anything to him and I won't have him come back out of obligation. I couldn't handle it. So it's best that he never knows. You raised me alone and I can raise this baby alone too."

She placed her finger on the butterfly pendant that Max had given to me. "Did he give this to you?"

I nodded my head as I continued to cry on her shoulder.

****

Thanksgiving came and went and it was time to fly back to New York. My mom and I had great conversations and I felt like a weight had been lifted off my shoulders. Danny, from what I could tell, was an amazing man and I could see why my mom was so in love with him. He treated her like a queen and she deserved nothing less. Watching the two of them over the past few days hit a sore spot with me because I missed Max so much. But it was time for me to forget about him and the time we shared and move on with my life; the life I was supposed to live when I moved to New York in the first place. Now it would be me plus one. Aubrey was graduating in a couple of weeks and then moving to New York. It was going to be great to have my three best friends by my side once again.

"Goodbye, Mom. Thanks again for everything." I gave a small smile as I hugged her.

"You call me if you need anything. I'll be in New York in a flash."

"Thanks, but I'll be okay. I promise."

"I'm going to miss watching your tummy grow." She pouted.

"Go get yourself an iPhone and we'll face time. Or learn how to use that computer of yours and we can skype."

Danny chuckled. "Don't worry, Emma. We're going to get her an iPhone right when we leave here. I don't want her missing a thing."

"Thanks, Danny." I hugged him tight. "Take care of her for me."

"You bet I will. I love this little lady."

My mom blushed. We gave one last hug and kiss and off I went, back home to New York to start my life on a fresh note. No more hiding in my apartment and away from life. This wasn't about me anymore.

Chapter 22

Five Months Later…

As I stood in the shower, I placed my hands on my rapidly growing belly. Last night was the first time I felt the baby kick. It was the most amazing feeling in the world, and the fact that another human being was growing inside of me had become more real. After showering, I got dressed and headed over to Kara and Molly's apartment. They both took the day off to accompany me to my ultrasound. Since Aubrey had court, she was going to try and meet us there. The three of them had been so supportive of me, and even though I still thought about Max, it started to hurt less every day. I sometimes questioned myself whether or not I made the right decision by not telling him about the baby. Feelings of guilt settled inside of me from time to time, but I had to remember that he had left for a reason. I was finishing up my second semester at Parsons and things were going well. I had the support of Hannah and Austin and our circle of friends grew. I kept waiting for the day when I'd run into Fiona or Max's parents. Thank God that hadn't happened yet, but I did have my story all made up and ready to be delivered when the time came. Kara had met a man named Billy and they had been seeing each other for about a month. Aubrey had been on a few dates with Glenn, one of the lawyers from her firm. Molly was still waiting for her Prince Charming to show up and I had sworn off all men.

I lay on the table with Molly, Kara, and Aubrey by my side as Dr. Richardson, my OB/GYN, pressed the wand across my abdomen. Seeing my baby at this stage for the first time brought tears to my eyes. That was my baby. The one person that I would nurture, love, and teach for the rest of my life.

"Would you like to know the sex?" he asked.

"Really? You know?" I asked in excitement.

"Yes. I can tell you now if you'd like."

I looked at the girls as they squeezed my hand and nodded their heads.

"Yes. I would like to know."

"Congratulations, Emma. You're going to have a daughter."

Tears started to fall from my eyes as everyone in the room squealed. "Oh my God, we're having a girl!" Molly exclaimed.

"She looks very healthy and she's growing right on schedule. I'll see you in a month for your checkup." He smiled as he left the room.

Kara took my hand and helped me up from the table. As happy as I was to find out that my baby was healthy, I was secretly excited that I was going to have a daughter. Having the girls with me made for a fun day, but I couldn't help feel a little sad that Max wasn't there to hear the news.

"Now that you know what the baby is, we can start working on the nursery." Aubrey smiled.

"Just think about how fun it's going to be to pick out girly things," Kara spoke.

****

I face timed my mom and held up the picture of the ultrasound. She started to cry when she saw it and even more when I told her she was going to have a granddaughter. Since the diner was short on waitresses, she couldn't get to New York like she wanted to, but she promised she'd be here when the baby was born. As I sat up in bed, I placed my headphones on my stomach and played some classical lullabies by Mozart while I read my book *What to Expect When You're Expecting*. My phone beeped, so I reached for it on the nightstand and my heart began to pound fiercely.

"I miss you, Emma."

I stared at those four words for a long time before I deleted his message. Why was he messaging me now? I wasn't going back down that road because I was finally healing and he wasn't going to fuck with my life or my heart ever again.

The next day, I met the girls for dinner at Carmine's on 44th Street. I had a huge craving for pasta and it couldn't be satisfied fast enough. When I walked in, they were already sitting in a booth, sipping on their wine.

"Hey." I smiled as I slid in next to Aubrey.

The waitress walked over and I ordered a water. "God, I can't wait to drink alcohol again. You're never going to believe what happened last night."

"What? Are you okay?" Aubrey asked with concern.

"Max sent me a text message telling me that he missed me."

"Shut up!" Molly exclaimed.

"What did you say to him?" Kara asked.

"Nothing. I deleted the message because I'm not responding."

Aubrey placed her hand on my arm. "Listen, Emma, and please don't get mad at me for saying this. You know how much

I love you and you're my very best friend. In fact, we're all like sisters. You never confessed your feelings to Max. You never told him that you loved him and that you wanted him to stay. You never had that talk with him before the planned break up. Maybe if you would have told him how you felt, things would be different."

"He knew, Aubrey. He even said in his letter that he knew he hurt me and he hoped that one day I could forgive him. He knew I was falling in love with him and he said he wasn't the man for me. He said he was flawed and I deserved someone flawless. His words, not mine. Why would he say that if he didn't know?"

"Maybe you're right and maybe the two of you need to talk. You are having his baby."

I began to get mad. What the fuck was Aubrey's problem? She was supposed to be on my side. Not his.

"So you're taking his side?" I snapped.

"No, Emma. I'm not taking anyone's side. I'm just saying the two of you need to talk about your feelings before you can just dismiss him from your life forever."

"Then he shouldn't have been such a coward and left me a letter."

"At least he gave you that. What if he just disappeared without saying a word?"

Kara and Molly sat across the table and didn't say anything. They just watched us talk back and forth while they ate their dinner.

"Do you agree with her?" I asked as I looked at them. "Well, do you?"

"Some of things she said make sense," Kara replied.

"I still think he's an asshole and I'm one hundred percent on your side, Emma," Molly chimed in.

"Thank you." I held up my glass of water. I sighed. Maybe Aubrey had a point.

"Listen, I get what you're saying, but I knew how he felt about relationships. He point blank told me he had no desire to be tied down to one woman for the rest of his life and play the happy little married couple with the perfect family. He said he didn't need some girl trying to control him. How would I have looked if I told him that I was falling in love with him? It would have made things awkward between us for the time we had left and he didn't give me a chance to say anything. I was going to tell him that morning how I felt." I wiped a tear that started to fall.

"It's not too late to tell him," Aubrey said as she grabbed my hand. "He said he missed you. That should say something."

"Things are different now. I'm over him and I have the baby to think about. I'm going to head home now. I'm really tired and my back is hurting."

Aubrey reached over and placed her arm around me, pulling me into her. "I'm sorry if I upset you. I'm just looking out for you."

"You didn't and I'm fine. I just need some time to think, that's all. I'll talk to you all later."

As I walked down the street, the window display at Baby Bellini caught my eye. I walked inside the boutique and over to the crib set that was displayed in the window; a mix of soft pink, gray, and white. It was love at first sight and the thought of mixing vintage-inspired accessories in the room flooded my mind. The kind saleslady and I talked for several minutes about the quality of the bedding as well as the crib that displayed it. There was no doubt in my mind that this was what I wanted. I purchased the bedding as well as the Simmons White Ambiance crib and matching Simmons White Ambiance double dresser. The bedding was available to take home and the furniture would be delivered in a couple of weeks. I left the store and stood on the sidewalk, trying to hail a cab with my large bags in hand. A black limousine pulled up and the passenger's window rolled down.

"Emma?"

I looked inside and swallowed hard.

"Darren. Hi."

He got out of the limo and walked around to the other side. He looked at my bulging stomach and then up at me. Tears formed in my eyes.

"Get in and I'll drive you home." He took the bags from me and put them in the trunk.

I slid into the backseat and thought of at least fifty lies to tell him.

"Is it his?" he asked as he pulled away from the curb.

"Yes." *There go my lies.* I couldn't lie to him. He was Darren and I always liked him. I always felt we had a special connection. "You can't tell him, Darren. Please," I pleaded.

"No worries, Emma. I won't."

He didn't say another word after that. Once he pulled up to my apartment building, he took my bags from the trunk and carried them upstairs to my apartment.

"You can set them on the floor. Thanks again. Would you like some coffee?" I asked.

He looked at his watch and then at me with a small smile. "Sure. I have some time before I have to pick up Mr. and Mrs. Delaney."

"Is that who you're working for now?"

He took a seat on the stool at the counter and interlaced his fingers. "I work for a lot of people now. When they need rides, they call me directly. How are you truly doing, Emma?"

"I'm okay." I set the coffee down in front of him. "Did you take Max to the airport that morning?"

He took a sip of his coffee and wrapped his hands around the mug. "Yes, I did, and believe me when I tell you that he was broken up. I'd never seen him like that before."

I rolled my eyes. "I doubt that. He left a letter, Darren. A damn letter."

"I know he did and I told him that it was the wrong thing to do and he should have spoken to you in person. But he's Max Hamilton and nobody tells him anything. You're not telling him about the baby?"

"There's no point now. I'm sure he's living his dream in Chicago and running his successful new business. The last thing he needs is to be tied down with the responsibility of a kid."

"What about your dream?"

"I'm living my dream one day at a time. I have great friends here who will help out and I have my classes. Believe it or not, Darren, things are really good," I lied. "Max sent me a text message last night, telling me that he missed me."

"I see. Remember when I told you when I first met you that sometimes people need to fall on their own in order to learn a valuable life lesson?"

"Yeah."

"I think Max fell the day he left that letter under your door."

"I don't know, but I can't worry about him anymore. If he wanted to stay and be with me, he would have."

He looked down at his coffee cup. "Do you know what you're having?"

I smiled. "I'm having a girl."

"Ah. She'll be just as beautiful as her mother. I better go. I don't want to be late picking up Mr. and Mrs. Delaney and then have them not hire me again."

"Thanks for the ride and the chat, Darren." I gave him a hug.

"Take care of yourself and that baby girl of yours. You have my number. Call me if you need anything at all."

"I will."

Chapter 23

Two Weeks Later...

The couple that bought the bedroom furniture from my other room were at my door bright and early to pick it up. They were newlyweds and looking for a used bedroom set for their spare room. The husband didn't really want it because he said it was for his mother-in-law when she came to visit. If they didn't have another bed, then she wouldn't stay with them. His wife politely told him that he'd be sleeping on the couch. I couldn't help but laugh. After they left, I stood in the middle of the empty room and looked around. The furniture was on back order and would be delivered within the week. This was the perfect time to get the walls painted. I decided to paint the wall with the window and the wall to the right a gray color that was called "Knitting Needles," and the opposite wall where the crib would sit a custom mix of two pinks: Cradle Pink and Almost Pink. I purchased the most adorable pink damask curtains that hung to the floor, matching the damask pattern on the bumper pads for the crib. I spent the whole day Saturday painting the ceiling, which killed my back, and the three walls. The ceiling was finished. Tomorrow, I'd put the second coat of paint on the walls. So far, it looked great and I was more than pleased. I didn't tell the girls that I was starting the nursery because this was a project I wanted to do on my own. Maybe tomorrow, I'd give them a call.

****

After eating breakfast, I sent a text message to Molly, asking her to stop by. Aubrey had plans for the day with Glenn, and Kara was going to New Jersey to meet Billy's parents. Molly texted me back, saying that she'd be over after work because she was doing hair for a wedding party. I changed into my jean overalls and my short-sleeve white shirt. I threw my hair up into a high ponytail and began putting the second coat of paint on the gray walls. After a couple of hours, all three walls were finished. I stood back and smiled as the sun filtered in through the blinds, brightening the room that was fit for a princess. There was a knock at the door and I looked at my phone. Molly must have gotten off early. I ran to the door in excitement for her to see what I'd done so far.

"I can't wait for you to see—" I started to say as I quickly opened the door.

I froze. My heart started pounding out of my chest and I felt sick to my stomach when I saw Max standing there. He looked at me and then at my belly. His eyes narrowed and he couldn't speak.

"Max, what are you doing here?" A tear was starting to form.

"I— I came to see you."

It was like time had stood still and the Earth had stopped spinning. *Shit. Shit. Shit.* He was nervous. I'd never seen him like this before.

"Come in," I said hesitantly.

"No. It's okay. I can see you're busy. I'm going to go." In that instant, I saw him break. He turned and started walking down the hallway.

Oh no, he doesn't. He's not walking away this time. "Max. The baby is yours. You're going to be a father," I blurted out in the open hallway.

He stopped dead in his tracks and waited a few moments before turning around. He slowly walked back to my door and stepped inside. The most awkward and scariest moment of my life was now happening.

"I thought you were Molly."

"Sorry to drop by unannounced, but you hadn't answered my text message, and I figured you wouldn't answer my calls either."

"You're right. I wouldn't have." I turned and walked to the kitchen and washed my hands under the warm water.

"Were you painting?" he asked as I had my back turned to him.

The emotions that were running through me were almost unbearable. I felt like it was getting harder to breathe.

"Yeah. I was painting the nursery." I took in a deep, long breath. I needed to remain calm for the baby's sake. I dried my hands on the towel, waiting for the question I knew was coming.

"Why didn't you tell me you were pregnant?"

And there it was. The question I had been waiting for.

"You were already gone." My voice quivered.

He took a seat at the table and placed his face in his hands. "You could have called." He slammed his fists down on the table and I flinched.

"And you could have told me goodbye in person. Not in the form of a fucking letter! You coward!" I screamed.

He ran his hand through his hair and lightly shook his head. "You can't be yelling like that or getting upset. It's not good for the baby. Please, Emma. Please come and sit down."

"I don't want to sit down! Who the hell do you think you are, coming back here to see me? I've moved on from you, Max. I got my shit together after you left and I'm doing what's right for my baby."

"OUR baby!" he spoke in anger.

"My baby! This is my baby!" I yelled as I walked over to him with a pointed finger. "I'm the one who's been sick every day and exhausted, barely making it through my classes. The one who's done all the shopping and planning and crying while trying to figure out how the hell I was going to raise a baby on my own while you were sitting in your plush luxury office in FUCKING Chicago!"

He got up and lightly took hold of my arm. "Emma, please."

"Don't. Don't you touch me!" I jerked away from him and crossed my arms, walking over to the window and staring out at the Hudson River. This was my go-to place when I needed to think.

"I left that note because I couldn't bear to look into your beautiful eyes and say goodbye. Do you think I enjoyed writing that letter? Do you think it made me happy? NO! I've been miserable in Chicago. I buried myself so deep into my work and company that I barely slept and when I did sleep, I dreamt of you. Every fucking night, Emma! You haunted my dreams. I tried to forget about you. I wanted to forget about you because the way I felt scared the fuck out of me."

I wiped the tears that fell down my face, but I still wouldn't turn around and look at him.

"I needed to get out of New York and away from my father. That was my plan all along. I didn't plan on falling for you. I knew the first time I met you at the club in Miami, I was already head over heels. I tried not to fall in love with you. Why the hell do you think you didn't see me every day? Why do you think I would let a week go by without seeing you? I was trying to stop my feelings, but it was too hard while we were both in New York. You were too close and I thought that maybe, just maybe moving to Chicago and not seeing you would help, but it didn't. The night I sent you that text message, I had been drinking. It was the only way I could muster up the courage to do it. When you didn't text me back, I was hurt but I understood because I knew I had hurt you by leaving the way I did. For fuck sakes, Emma. Will you turn around and look at me?"

I slowly turned around and stared at the wounded man across the room who possessed the same look I once had and maybe still had.

"I spent too many months trying to forget you. You have no idea how scared and alone I was," I spewed.

"I'm sorry. Can we please, at least for tonight, just push all the anger away and talk? Just talk and catch up?" he spoke in a lowered voice. "I would do anything to change the past. I'm so sorry, Emma. You have to believe me."

The truth was that I did believe him and being angry wasn't helping the baby. "Fine. Let's talk then."

"Can I see the nursery?"

"You know where it's at."

He walked in the room and flipped the light on the wall. "Pink? Does that mean we're going to have a little girl?"

"Yep. I'd be really concerned if it was a boy if I were you."

He let out a light chuckle. "A daughter. I can't believe I'm going to have a daughter. I like how you painted these two walls gray. Did you do this all by yourself?"

"Yeah. The furniture is coming next week and I've already bought some things for the walls and I still have to hang the curtains."

"When are you due?" He looked over at me.

"Eight weeks."

"I'm sorry I have to ask this, but how did this happen?"

"Really, Max?"

"I don't mean it like that. You were on the pill."

"I know and there were days when I forgot, but I always doubled up the next day or two. I'm sorry."

"Don't be sorry. I'm not mad. I'm a little scared, but not mad."

I walked to my room and took the ultrasound picture from my dresser and handed it to Max. "Meet your daughter. You can keep that. I have another one."

He stared at her with such intensity and I could see the water creep up in his eyes. "She's beautiful, Emma."

I felt a kick and flinched, placing my hand on my belly.

"What's wrong?" Max asked in a startled voice.

"She kicked. She likes to do that."

"May I?" He held out his hand.

I nodded.

He placed the palm of his hand on my belly and held it there. His touch, which I had longed for and my body craved, sent my body into overdrive. She kicked again and Max felt it. A smile crossed his lips as he looked into my eyes.

"Oh my God. That is incredible."

I brought my hand and placed it on his.

"Emma," he whispered. "I—"

I pulled back. "Don't, Max. I don't think I can do this. You need to leave."

"I don't want to leave you again. You have no idea how much I've missed you."

I turned away because I couldn't look in his eyes anymore. The sadness was overwhelming and I was confused.

"No, I don't and I don't want to know. These past five months have been unbearable, but every day that you weren't here, I grew stronger. Not only for me, but for the baby. You just can't walk back into my life and expect things to be the same. You hurt me on such a level that I don't know if I could ever trust you again. The only thing we share is a child."

"Were you ever going to tell me about her?"

"I don't know. Maybe someday I was going to. But you have to understand that you left. You started a new life, a new company, and I wasn't about to ruin that for you by telling you about her."

"But I'm her father. I have a right to know that she exists!" he yelled.

"I wasn't about to let you ruin her life like your father did yours." I slowly closed my eyes. I spoke the words that would hurt him the most.

"That's low, Emma. Even for you. If you want me to leave, then fine. I'll leave. But this isn't over." He turned and walked out the door, slamming it shut behind him.

I flinched as I stood in the middle of the nursery and sobbed. I heard the door open and Molly came walking into the nursery.

"Emma, I just saw Max in the lobby." She wrapped her arms around me.

"He just thinks he can walk back into my life like nothing ever happened."

Chapter 24

A week passed and I didn't hear a word from Max. But then again, that was his usual style, so I wasn't surprised. I finished up the last semester of school and ended it with a 3.8 GPA. The nursery was finished and the furniture was set to be delivered this afternoon. I couldn't wait to get it all set up. I had purchased a chandelier from Pottery Barn Kids with sweeping scrolls, life-like candles, and sparkling crystals. The maintenance man from the building, Jim, put it up for me and replaced the existing ceiling light that was already there.

As I was unwrapping some of the accessories I bought, there was a knock at the door. I looked out the peephole to see if it was the deliverymen. My heart started pounding when I saw Max standing there. I hesitantly opened the door and he came barging in without so much as a "hi."

"I just wanted you to know that I'm moving my business from Chicago to New York so I can be near my daughter. I will be in her life, Emma. You cannot stop me from seeing her. You can hate me all you want, but I will be here for her. And regardless of what you think, I will not ruin her life. I will not make the same mistakes my parents did."

As I stood there and listened to him and his raised voice, there was another knock on the door. I turned around and opened it.

"We have a furniture delivery for a Miss Emma Knight."

"Yes. Come in. I'll show you where it goes."

Max placed his hands in his pockets and stood over by the window, looking out at the view while the two men brought in the furniture and placed it in the nursery. The first was a large cardboard box with the crib in it. The second was the double dresser with the hutch and the third was a glider and ottoman I had purchased in Valetti Silver.

"If you'll sign here, we'll be on our way."

I signed the form and thanked the deliverymen. As soon as they left, Max turned around and looked at me.

"Do you have anything to say?"

"Okay. A little girl needs her daddy in her life. I didn't have that and I don't want that for my daughter. If you want to be involved, then we'll have to make it work. You can be involved in her life but not in mine."

A sharply distressed look swept across his face. "If that's the way you want it, then fine."

"Fine," I said.

I walked into the nursery and looked at the cardboard box sitting against the wall. I sighed.

"Is that the crib in there?" Max asked.

"Yes. I sort of thought they would have delivered it built."

Max walked over to it and asked for a pair of scissors.

"What are you doing?" I asked.

"I'm going to put this crib together so we need to get it out of the box."

I busted out into laughter.

"What's so funny? You don't think I can do it?"

"Honestly, no. I don't."

He gave me a small smile. "It's going to give me great pleasure to prove you wrong, Emma. Now please get me some scissors so I can open this up and get started."

I shook my head and walked into the kitchen to fetch a pair of scissors from the drawer. I handed them to him and took a seat in the glider, putting my feet up on the ottoman.

"That's a nice chair," he commented.

"Thanks. I saw it and couldn't resist."

He laid the box down and opened it, taking out the directions and the overly huge plastic bag with a million screws and springs in it. I smirked. He pulled out the directions and began reading them over. His face tightened.

"It says we need a screwdriver, hammer, pliers, and a ratchet set. Do you have those things?"

"No." I smiled.

"Well then, I guess we're making a trip to the hardware store and buying them. Get your shoes on. I'll call Darren and have him come pick us up."

"Darren? He's working for you again?" I asked as I got up from the glider.

"Yes. He's working for me full-time again and I've given him a large raise." He pulled his phone out and gave Darren a call. "He'll be here in about ten minutes. I should bring these directions with us."

This was going to be fun. Watching him trying to build the baby's crib was something I'd have to record. "Have you ever built anything before?"

"No. But how hard can it be? The directions seem simple enough."

"Okay. If you say so." I smirked as I slipped on my shoes and we headed out the door.

When we walked out of the building, Darren was standing at the curb next to the Rolls Royce. I smiled and gave him a light hug.

"Drop us off at the closest hardware store. What's that place called? Home Department or something?"

I laughed and Darren smiled at me from the rearview mirror.

"You mean Home Depot?" I lightly smacked his arm.

"I guess."

We walked through Home Depot and I could tell that Max had no clue what he was doing or where he was going.

"See the large signs throughout the store? They tell you which department you're in. And see the signs at the end of each aisle? They tell you what kind of items are down that aisle."

"Ah, I didn't notice those."

I laughed again. Finally, after an hour in the store, we found the tools we needed and then had to stop in the drill section so Max could play with them. "I think I'll buy one of these."

"For what?"

"You never know when you'll need one and they're pretty cool."

****

As I planted my tired self back in the ottoman, Max removed all the pieces to the crib and sat down in the middle of the cluttered floor. Watching him look over the directions and trying to figure out which piece was which was funny but also amazingly sweet.

"Do you need some help?" I asked.

"Would you like to help?"

"Sure. If you weren't here, I would be doing it anyway." I got up and sat down next to him on the floor and studied the diagram. About halfway through building it, he stopped and looked at me.

"I think this piece is on backwards."

"I think you're right. Listen, we've been doing this for three hours and I'm starving. This little one wants to eat." I placed both hands on my belly.

"I'm starving too. How about some Thai food?"

"That sounds great."

He got up and held out his hand to help me up from the floor. The minute I placed mine in his, an overwhelming feeling washed over me. He helped me up and we walked to the kitchen, where I took the menu from the side of the fridge. After deciding what we wanted, Max called in the order for delivery. I grabbed a bottle of water from the refrigerator and sat down at the table.

"Have you seen your father?" I asked.

"Yes, and it didn't go over well. He pretty much disowned me. His words." He sat down across from me.

"Why?" To think that a parent would disown their child saddened me, and I couldn't even imagine it.

"He told me I betrayed him and he doesn't deal with traitors. We got into a huge fight and my mom just stood there and didn't say a word. He told me to watch my back with my company because it could all come crashing down in the blink of an eye."

"Max, I'm sorry."

"He's a ruthless son of a bitch. He always has been and he always will be. He told me that I was no longer a part of the family and he never wanted to see me again."

"And your mom just stood by and let him talk to you like that?"

"Yep. I walked out of their house and I don't have any intention of ever going back."

"Are you going to tell them about the baby?"

"No, Emma. I'm no longer a part of their family, so, technically, they aren't going to have a grandchild."

"What about Fiona?"

"I'll tell her. She hates them and she's flying to Paris for the summer. She said she may not come back."

"What about college?"

"She'll study over there."

My heart ached for him. It truly did because I could see the sadness in his eyes and the despair in his voice when he talked about them. This had to be incredibly hard for him. There was a knock at the door and Max got up and answered it and set our food on the table. I took a couple of plates down and set the table. As we sat there eating, I asked him about his company.

"Where are you going to set up here in New York?"

"Connor Black of Black Enterprises has the third floor of his building for rent. I met with him earlier in the week and signed the agreement. It'll do for now until the company grows. Then I can move to my own building."

"What's your company called?" I asked out of curiosity.

"Hamilton Tech. I've hired the best of the best to develop new software and hi tech equipment that people are going to love. Or at least I hope they do."

"They will." I gave a small smile.

After we finished eating, it was back to building the crib. Many expletives later and two more hours, it was finally built and put in its proper place.

"Good job, Hamilton." I put my hand on his shoulder.

"I couldn't have done it without your help."

I opened up the closet and took out the large bag that held some of the wall hangings. I pulled out the silver letter S and held it up.

"What's that?" Max asked.

"Her first initial."

"You've picked a name?"

"Sarah. Sarah Renee Hamilton. The meaning of Sarah is princess."

Without even thinking about it, he walked over and wrapped his arms around me, pulling me into him. Or at least as much as he could without my belly getting in the way. I didn't pull back because it felt so good to be held again.

"I love that name and she truly will be a princess. I wasn't sure if you were going to give her my last name."

"Well, I wasn't going to at first, but since you're back and you've made it very clear that you're going to be in her life, I thought I'd better. She should have the Hamilton name."

"Thank you, Emma. You have no idea what that means to me." He kissed the top of my head.

"I bought something else." I broke our embrace and pulled two silver butterflies from the bag.

He smiled.

"I always want our little girl to dance. Even on her saddest days."

"She will. She'll have your strength and, with you as her mother, she'll dance her whole life. Would you like me to hang them?"

"Yes. Please."

He hung the oval silver mirror first and then the butterflies on each side. It was perfect.

"I better get going. You look exhausted and it's getting late," he spoke.

"Okay. Thank you for everything today."

"You're welcome, Emma. Thank you too."

I gave him a smile as I walked him to the door. "I'll be in touch. I promise."

"Bye, Max."

"Bye, Emma. Bye, Sarah." He placed his hand on my belly.

Chapter 25

"Emma, how are you? Are you okay? Is the baby okay?"

"Mom. Calm down. I called to say hi. Everything is fine."

I heard her sigh. "Thank God. You know I get very nervous every time I see your name pop up."

"I have something to tell you, Mom. Max is back in New York and he knows about the baby. He told me that he wants to be in her life. So…"

"Are you okay?"

"Yeah, Mom. I'm okay."

"It's best that he's in her life. You know that, right? You didn't get to grow up with a father and you didn't have a choice. My granddaughter has a choice because her father wants to be in her life. It's the best gift you can give her."

"I know. Listen, Mom, I have to go now. I'll talk to you soon."

As I sat on the mushroom and looked up at the bright blue sky, I took in the warmth of the sun upon my skin. Watching the mothers pushing their babies in their strollers, I smiled because, before too long, that would be me and Sarah. The girls were happy that Max was taking responsibility for his daughter, but Molly still wasn't convinced. She said a man like him doesn't change overnight. Who knows? Maybe they do or maybe they don't. I hadn't heard from Max in a few days and I was okay with that. We were friends who were sharing a child. My phone rang and when I looked at the screen, I saw that Max was calling. I smiled.

"Hello."

"Hi."

"Hi."

"Are you home?"

"No."

"Where are you?"

"Sitting on a mushroom in Central Park." I smiled.

"Ah. Alice In Wonderland. Stay there. I'm on my way."

"Why?"

"You'll see. Be there soon."

Hannah and I were texting each other back and forth and, when I looked up, I saw Max walking towards me. My heart fluttered every time I saw him in one of his business suits.

"Smile." He held up his phone and snapped a picture of me. He held out his hand and helped me up.

"So, to what do I owe the pleasure of being in your company today, Mr. Hamilton?"

"Sorry I've been MIA the past few days. I've been getting things moved from Chicago and to my new office."

"That's good. I'm surprised you're not at the office now."

"I was, but I really want you to see it, so that's why I called you. I thought maybe we could go to my office and then go to lunch. Plus, I saw this really cool stroller in the window at Baby Bellini that I wanted to show you."

I gave him a small smile. "That sounds like fun."

"Great. Let's go." He held out his arm.

We walked to the Rolls Royce where Darren was waiting for us and he drove us to Max's office. We walked into the lobby of Black Enterprises and took the elevator up to the third floor.

When the doors opened, we were greeted by a woman with long, black hair, a slender waist, and legs that any woman would die for. Not to mention the fact that when you looked at her, all you saw was her cleavage. It made me very insecure.

"Hello, Mr. Hamilton."

"Hello, Brazil." He smiled.

I rolled my eyes as he led me to his office. He pushed open the large dark wood doors and we stepped inside. In front of the wall of windows sat a long, rectangular glass desk with a black executive chair behind it.

"This is great, Max. It suits you." I winked. "It's very corporate."

"I'm glad you approve, considering I'm a corporate man."

I walked around his desk and noticed the double picture frame sitting on it. On the left side was me sitting in the ottoman in the nursery, looking out the window with my hand on my belly, and on the right side was the ultrasound picture I gave him.

"When did you take this picture of me? I look horrible."

"The day we built the crib, and I think you look beautiful. Do you have a problem with me having your picture on my desk? You are the mother of my child."

"You don't think it's a bit odd since we're not together?" I arched my eyebrow.

"No. That's you pregnant and our baby girl on the other side. What's so odd about that?"

I sighed. I wasn't about to get in an argument over it. "Nothing." I set the picture frame down on the desk and quickly changed the subject. "Brazil? Really?"

"What about her?" he asked.

"I take it that cleavage is part of your employee dress code."

He chuckled. "She's not my type."

"What is your type?" I asked unwillingly.

He placed his hands on my hips. "I didn't even know I had one until I met you." His eyes stared into mine.

I gulped. "Why don't we head over to Baby Bellini and you can show me that really cool stroller."

He brought his finger up to my chin and then lightly ran it across my jawline. His eyes were seductive and his lips were dangerously close to mine as he leaned in closer to me. I broke our moment. I knew he was about to kiss me and I couldn't let it happen. I was a hormonal mess and very vulnerable.

"We better go." I walked towards the door and I heard him sigh.

We stepped inside Baby Bellini and, instantly, the saleslady recognized me.

"Hello there. Did your furniture get delivered on time?" she asked with a smile.

"Yes, and it's just as beautiful in the nursery as it was in your window display."

"We're here to look at that stroller you have in the window," Max spoke.

"Ah, yes. That's our new arrival. Come with me and I'll show the special features."

Suddenly, I felt like we were buying a car.

"As you can see, the seat is reversible and it's a simple one-step fold. This stroller is the only one you'll ever need. The shock and suspension is unlike any other stroller, which makes for a smooth ride. It will keep baby very happy and a happy baby makes for happy parents." She grinned. "It also comes with this bassinet, which attaches right here. Easy on, easy off."

I glanced at the price tag. It was eight hundred dollars.

"What do you think, Emma?" Max asked.

"I think it's great but a little on the expensive side for a stroller."

"But, honey, your baby will be so comfortable in it. It also has an extra-large basket for the diaper bag and any other bags you may have. And the sunshade is extendable to shield that precious little one from the sun."

"Sounds good to me. We'll take it." Max smiled.

As soon as the Max paid for the stroller, he turned and looked at me. "Are you ready for lunch?"

"Do you think you can take me home? I'm not feeling well."

"What's wrong?" he asked with concern.

"My stomach hurts a bit and I just want to lie down."

"Of course. Let's get you home right away."

****

I stepped inside the apartment and walked straight to my bedroom and lay on the bed. Max walked in and set a bottle of water on the nightstand.

"Thanks."

"You're welcome. Do I need to call your doctor?" he asked as he placed his hand on my forehead.

"No. I think I just need to sleep for a while."

"Okay. I'll be out there if you need anything."

"You're staying?"

"Yeah. I'm not leaving you alone. I have some work to do, so I'll just sit on the couch and do it. Now close your eyes." He smiled.

A couple of hours later, I awoke to a severe cramping in my stomach. Cramping so bad that I could barely breathe.

"MAX!" I screamed.

Within a second, he came running into the room. "What's wrong?" He leaned over me.

"I don't know. I'm cramping really bad. Something's wrong."

He pulled his phone from his pocket and called Darren to get here as fast as he could. "I'm taking you to the hospital."

Tears were streaming down my face as I tried to get up with Max's help.

"Come on, sweetheart. Everything's going to be okay."

"No, Max. Something's wrong." I doubled over and he grabbed me.

"Okay. Let's just get you to the hospital."

I struggled to get down to the lobby. The pain was intense. I slid into the back seat, and as soon as Max climbed in next to me, I laid my head on his shoulder and he took hold of my hand. Darren pulled up to the emergency entrance and Max flew out of the car and ran inside, getting a nurse to come outside.

"What's going on, honey?" the blonde-haired woman asked. "How far along are you?"

"Twenty-eight weeks and I'm cramping really bad."

"Okay. Let's get you out of the car and up to the labor and delivery unit."

She helped me out of the car while Max held the wheelchair and I sat down.

"How far apart are the cramps?" the nurse asked.

"They're constant."

As she wheeled me up, Max held my hand. Once we arrived to the labor and delivery unit, I was immediately put into a room and two nurses helped me into a gown and quickly hooked me up to the fetal monitor. I looked at Max and grabbed his arm.

"You need to call the girls and tell them I'm here."

"I will in a bit. Let's wait and see what the doctor says."

Within minutes, Dr. Richardson walked in the room. "I'm glad I was here, Emma. What's going on?"

"I think I'm in labor, Dr. Richardson, and it's way too soon."

He put my feet in the stirrups and looked at Max.

"It's okay. He's the baby's father."

Dr. Richardson nodded and examined me. He looked at me and pursed his lips. "It's time, Emma. We need to do a C-Section now."

I looked at Max and shook my head as my lips trembled and the tears ran down my face. "No. It's too soon."

"We don't have a choice." The door flew open and two men came in with a gurney. They helped me from the bed and rushed me down the hall and into the operating room. Max followed behind and changed into scrubs and a mask. As I lay there while the nurses prepped me, horrific thoughts flooded my mind. It was too soon and I wasn't prepared for what might happen to her.

"It's okay," Max spoke as he pressed my hand against his lips.

"I'm making the incision, Emma," Dr. Richardson said.

"Just look at me," Max softly spoke. "She's going to be fine. You have to believe that."

He was trying so hard to stay strong for me, but I could tell he was about to break. He held my hand and, for a moment, buried his face in my shoulder.

"Get her to the NICU stat," Dr. Richardson yelled at the nurses as he handed them Sarah. "She's about two pounds, Emma, and we have to get her to the NICU."

"Can't I see her?" I cried.

"I'm sorry, but not yet. We have to get her the proper medical care immediately."

My mind couldn't wrap itself around the fact that my baby was born two months early. What did I do wrong? Could I have prevented this? Random questions flooded my mind as I turned away from Max because I couldn't bear looking at how distraught he was. He didn't say a word and he didn't have to. I didn't want him to.

Dr. Richardson finished stitching me up and walked over and placed his hand on mine.

"Your little girl is in the best hands and is getting the best care. With today's medical advances, babies born this early have way better survival rates than they did ten years ago. Plus, she's a girl and girls are strong." He winked. "You've been through an ordeal today and you need to rest. Not only for your baby, but for your body to start healing. It's important, Emma, that you get as much rest as possible. You have to be strong for your daughter."

I nodded my head as tears continued to fall from my eyes. He walked out of the room and the nurses wheeled me back to mine. After getting me settled, a different nurse walked in.

"Hi, Emma, my name is Lila and I'm going to be taking care of you for the rest of my shift. I'm going to give you a little something to help you relax." She pushed a needle into my IV line. "I promise to keep you both updated on your daughter."

Before I knew it, my eyes had closed and I was fast asleep.

Chapter 26

My eyes opened, and Max wasn't in the room. Nobody was in the room but me. I was in pain. The numbing medication must have worn off and I was feeling it big time. As I lay there, flat on my back, looking up at the ceiling, the fear for my daughter's life overwhelmed me and the tears started up again. A few moments later, Max walked in and came to my bedside.

"Hey," he said as he ran his thumb across my forehead.

"Hey." I swallowed hard.

"I called Kara and she was going to tell Molly and Aubrey. They'll be here later. They wanted to come now and I told them that you needed to rest first. They also said they would call your mom."

"Have you seen her?" I asked.

He looked down and softly nodded.

"And?" I spoke sharply.

"She's doing as well as can be expected and she's beautiful. I talked to the specialist and he'll be in to talk to you soon."

"What did he say?"

Just then, a man who appeared to be in his forties with sandy brown long hair and green eyes stepped into the room.

"Hi, Emma. I'm Dr. Cooper and I'll be taking care of Sarah. I know what you're going through right now both emotionally and physically, but I want you to know that the outlook for Sarah is good. Her heart is perfect and she looks as good as can be expected for a twenty-eight-week-old preemie. I don't see any abnormalities at all. The only problem is her breathing is a little unstable and we have her hooked up to a ventilator to help her. This is common in babies born this early and I don't want you to be alarmed. I have a special team of nurses that are the best in the field and they're going to take care of her around the clock."

"When can I see her?"

"As soon as you're able to get out of bed. Probably tomorrow. I know it's hard, but try to focus on healing yourself because I won't lie to you. This is going to be one of the toughest and most exhausting journeys you will ever face, and you need to be at your best and one hundred percent. Sarah is fighting and she's going to need you to help her." He gave a small smile. "I'm going to go back and check on her and I'll talk to you both soon. Until then, rest up."

After Dr. Cooper left, Lila, the nurse, walked in. "Did you have a nice nap?" She smiled. "I see you've met Dr. Cooper. He's one of the top neonatal doctors in the country. We are so fortunate to have him working here. Your daughter is in the best hands. Do you need some more pain medication?"

"Yes, please."

"Okay. I'll be right back."

"Can I get you anything, Emma?" Max kindly asked.

"Maybe some water?"

He took the cup from the table and brought the straw up to my lips. I slowly took a few sips. He sat down in the chair and took hold of my hand.

"I believe Sarah is going to be just fine. She's a fighter like her mom."

"I hope so because if anything happens to her, Max, it'll destroy me."

"I know, baby. But she'll be fine."

"Don't you think you should tell your parents?"

"I don't want to talk about that right now and I don't want you thinking about them."

I turned my head and looked out the window. I didn't want to talk, period. Lila walked back in and pushed the pain meds through my IV.

"There you go. You should start feeling some relief soon. Try to get some more rest and, first thing tomorrow morning, we'll get you up and walking around. If you need anything, just press this button."

I looked over at Max, who was checking his phone. "Is something wrong?" I asked.

"No. I was just looking over some emails."

"You don't have to stay, Max. I know you're busy."

He gave me a look of disappointment. "How could you even say that? Sarah is my child too and I'm not going to abandon her. I don't care how busy I am. I have people that can handle work at the office for me while I'm gone."

He was extremely upset when I said that and it hadn't been my intention to upset him. There was nothing he could do here and he had a business to run.

"Max, I'm sorry. It's just that you don't need to sit here with me. You have a company to run and I don't want it to suffer."

"Don't worry about my company, Emma. I'm staying right where I belong and that's here with you and our daughter."

I turned away because I couldn't look at him. I blamed myself for Sarah being born early and if something happened to her, he would never forgive me and I would never forgive myself.

****

Despite me telling Max to go home last night, he stayed and slept on a cot in the room next to my bed. The morning nurse, Kayla, walked in and told me that I had to get up and try to walk around.

"I need to see my baby," I said with desperation.

"Okay. Let me just call down and tell them you're coming."

As soon as she walked out of the room, Max took hold of both my hands. "Listen, Emma, I want you to be prepared when you go and see her. She's hooked up to different machines and tubes and I don't want you to be scared."

"I know."

"No, baby, you don't. It's one thing to think about it and another when you actually see it."

Kayla walked back in the room with a wheelchair. "Are you ready?"

I took in a deep, long breath and sat down in the chair. Max told the nurse that he would take me and bring me back to the room. We approached the neonatal unit and got buzzed in. My heart began to beat rapidly as he pushed me down the hallway and to the large room where Sarah was. The room was so cold and the beeping sounds of the high-calibrated machines were the only sounds I could hear. The sounds that were keeping all the sick and premature babies alive.

"You must be Emma. I'm Laney and I've been taking care of Sarah." She gave me a sympathetic smile.

I nodded my head, unable to speak from the lump in my throat that was constricting my breathing as fear swept throughout my body. Max pushed the wheelchair up to the incubator where my baby girl lay helpless with a tube down her tiny little throat, helping her breathe. I placed my hand over my mouth as the tears fell down my face and I began to sob uncontrollably. Max knelt down beside me and wrapped his arm around me.

"I know it's hard, but she's going to be okay."

I felt as if I was hyperventilating. Seeing her so helpless and fighting for her life was too much. I couldn't take it. I had to leave.

"Take me back to the room, Max," I cried as I shook uncontrollably.

"Emma."

"Take me back now!"

He looked at Laney, the nurse, and I heard her say that this was completely normal and that it would take a bit of time for me to adjust to seeing her like that. Max stood up and wheeled me back to the room. I was hysterical and couldn't stop crying. This wasn't fair to Sarah and it was all my fault. As I climbed back into the bed, Kayla came in and pushed some medication through my IV.

"This is going to help you relax and calm down, Emma. Don't fight it."

Max held my hand and stared at me with tears in his eyes as I slowly closed mine and drifted to sleep.

Chapter 27

I awoke to the sounds of whispering. When I opened my eyes, I saw my mom standing over me.

"Emma," she said with tears in her eyes.

"Mom. What are you doing here?"

"I took the first flight out of Miami. I needed to be here for my girls. I'm so sorry you're going through this." She sat on the edge of the bed and placed her hand on my cheek. "Sarah is going to be just fine. She's going to pull through this. She's a Knight and we Knight women are fighters."

"You met Max?"

"Yes." She smiled at him.

Max walked over to the other side of the bed. "You need to eat something. I took the liberty of ordering your dinner because you were asleep. If you want me to go get you something else, I will."

"I'm not hungry. I can't eat."

"Emma, you have to. You have to keep your strength up for your daughter," my mom spoke.

"Now that your mom is here, I'm going to step outside and make a few phone calls." He leaned over and kissed my forehead and walked out of the room.

"That man loves you, Emma."

"Mom. I don't want to talk about him right now. I totally freaked out when I saw her lying in that incubator. I didn't want to be there. I wanted to get away as fast as I could. What kind of mother am I?" I began to sob.

"The kind of mother who is scared to death for her child. Emma, you have to believe that she's going to pull through. If you don't have hope or faith, then neither does she."

"It's so hard seeing her like that. I don't know if I can do this. I'm not strong enough."

"Nonsense. Now you listen to me. You are strong and you will be strong for that little girl. Remember what I always told you: God doesn't give us more than we can handle. If God didn't think you could do this, then he would have already taken her."

There was a knock on the door and, when it opened, a young girl walked in with my dinner tray and set it on my table. She gave me a small smile and, as she walked out, Max walked back in. My mom took the lid off and stared at the chicken breast that lay on the plate.

"Good choice, Max." She smiled.

"You can't go wrong with chicken, right?"

"Let's hope not." She winked.

I took a couple of bites and pushed it away. "I'm not hungry."

I felt broken beyond repair. I was helpless to my daughter and my emotions were all over the place. After a few hours, my mom looked tired and I told her to go to my apartment and get some rest. The truth was that I just wanted to be alone.

"I'm going to take your mom back to your place. Do you need me to get you anything while I'm there?"

"Can you bring me my pink nightgown and matching robe that's hanging on the bathroom door? My hairbrush, toothbrush, rubber bands, deodorant."

He smiled. "Of course I can. I'll be back in a while. Are you going to be okay?"

"Yeah. I just want to be alone for a while."

My mom lightly hugged me and kissed my head. "I'll see you tomorrow morning, sweetheart."

"Bye, Mom."

As soon as they left, I lay there; confused, helpless, and overwhelmed. Lila was back on shift and when she walked into the room, she smiled at me.

"Have you been up and around?"

"Not really. I've been asleep most of the day."

"Well, come on, Emma. Let's do this."

"I can't," I said as I turned my head.

"Yes, you can and you will. You aren't getting a pity party from me. You're going to get up and you're going to walk around. You're going to get stronger and then you're going to help that little girl of yours."

She helped me up from the bed and lightly held on to me as I slowly walked up and down the hall. About two hours later, Max returned and set my bag on the chair in the corner.

"How are you?" he asked as he walked over to the bed.

"I need a shower."

"Are you allowed?"

"Yeah, but I'm going to need your help because I can't lift my arms to wash my hair."

"Of course I'll help you."

Suddenly, the raw emotion of him seeing me naked terrified me. The last time he saw me, I was slender and toned.

"You know what? Forget it. I can take it some other time."

"Why? I think taking a shower will help you feel a little better. Maybe even clear your mind a bit."

"No. It's okay." I crossed my arms over my chest.

He gave me a strange look and narrowed his eye. "Are you afraid to be naked in front of me? Have you forgotten that I've seen all of you and that's what got us here in the first place?"

"No. I haven't forgotten. But the last time you saw me naked, I was thin and we were having sex."

"It doesn't matter. You were beautiful then and you're just as beautiful now."

"I know this may sound crazy to you but sometimes, when I look at you, I feel like you're a stranger."

"I'm sorry, Emma. I truly am. Please let me help you. Please."

"Fine."

He helped me to the bathroom and closed the door. He turned on the water and made sure it was nice and hot, but not too hot. He rolled up his sleeves and untied the back of my gown, taking it off of me and setting it on the sink. He didn't look at me any differently than he used to. I stepped into the tub and stood there as he removed the handheld showerhead and let it run down my blonde hair.

"I brought your shampoo and conditioner. I left it in the bag. Hold this and I'll be right back."

A few seconds later, he entered the bathroom with my bottles of shampoo and conditioner from home. He poured some in his hand and slowly massaged it into my hair. Oh my God, his fingers felt so good on my scalp. After rinsing, he ran some conditioner through my hair and then helped me wash my body.

"Did my mom get settled okay?"

"Yeah. She's a great woman, Emma. You're lucky to have her as a mother."

"Thanks. She is pretty awesome."

"Darren sends his love. He said he'll stop by tomorrow if you're feeling up to it."

"That would be great."

Once my shower was finished, I stepped out and Max wrapped the towel around me. After changing into my nightgown and robe, I walked over to the bed and sat down.

"I want to see her again, Max."

"Now?"

"Yeah."

"Maybe you should wait until the morning."

I shook my head. "No. I want to see her now."

"Okay. I'll go grab a wheelchair."

"I can walk."

"Are you sure?"

"Yeah."

We went to the neonatal unit and walked into the cold room. Laney, the nurse I met earlier, smiled when she saw me.

"You're back."

"I'm sorry about earlier."

She placed her hand on my shoulder. "Don't apologize. It's hard to see your baby like that the first time.

I walked over to where she was lying and Laney pulled up a chair. I sat down as a few tears filled my eyes.

"You can touch her." Laney smiled.

"Really?" I looked up at her.

"Babies need their mother's touch and she can hear you too, so make sure to talk to her. Trust in your abilities to start parenting. She needs you now more than ever."

I placed my hand through the large hole of the incubator and felt the warmth on my skin as my finger softly stroked her little hand.

"She's beautiful." I began to cry as I looked up at Max.

"I know she is. Would it be wrong of me to say she's the most beautiful baby in this hospital?"

I let out a light laugh. "When will I be able to hold her?" I asked Laney.

"Probably in a couple of days. She's doing really well and she may be able to come off the ventilator soon. She is a little anemic, which is common in babies born this early, so tomorrow morning, we're going to give her a blood transfusion. It's nothing to worry about and just about every baby in here has had one. I'll leave the two of you alone to visit with your daughter. If you need anything, I'll be right across the room."

As I stared at Sarah and stroked her tiny arm, I still couldn't believe that she was here. Max knelt down next to me and I removed my hand so he could touch her.

"Go ahead." I gave a small smile.

When he touched her hand, she splayed her little fingers. "She moved." He smiled.

I laid my head on his shoulder as I stared at my beautiful tiny baby girl. We took turns touching and comforting her until Laney told us that we had to leave because they were about to do a shift change. We walked back to the room and I could tell how tired Max was.

"I want you to go home, Max. You need to get some proper sleep in your own bed."

"I'm fine, Emma."

"Seriously, Max. Go. I'm fine and you can come back first thing tomorrow morning. I'll wait for you to go and see her."

"Are you sure?"

"I'm positive."

"All right then. I'll be here first thing in the morning." He leaned over and kissed my head.

As soon as he left the room, I lay down and buzzed the nurse for some more pain meds. Max and I had a long road ahead of us as far as Sarah was concerned. He was so attentive to me and my needs and a feeling of confusion settled inside of me. I kept thinking about my father and how he just left us without any explanation at all. As I lay there, I heard the sounds of the crying babies who were with their mothers in their rooms.

I stayed in the hospital a couple of more days and, on my last day there, I was able to hold my little girl for a few minutes. When the nurse put her in my arms, I began to cry when she opened her eyes and looked at me. Dr. Cooper had walked over to us and told us how well she was doing and that tomorrow they would be taking her off the ventilator. The hardest part was yet to come. The moment I had to step outside the hospital doors and leave my daughter behind. My mom stayed with me the entire day yesterday and then had to catch a flight back to Miami to go back to work at the diner. They were down a waitress because Maureen's husband had passed away.

Max and I went back to my room and the nurse brought in the discharge papers for me to sign.

"Since you don't have any insurance, we'll need a partial payment today," she spoke.

"I will pay for Emma's stay, but my daughter is covered under my insurance plan through my company."

She nodded and left the room.

"Max, you don't need to do that."

"Yes, I do. Now no arguing. Are you ready to go home?"

"No. I'm not," I replied as I walked over to the window and stared out into the courtyard.

He walked over and placed his hands on my shoulders. "I know how hard this is because I'm feeling it too, but we have no choice."

I sighed. "I know."

Darren had come up and taken the flowers that my friends sent me down to the car while Max grabbed my bag. We were supposed to wait for a wheelchair, hospital policy, but I didn't want to go down in one. I was more than capable of walking.

Chapter 28

Max and I looked like ordinary people walking out of the hospital. We didn't appear to be new parents, holding our baby and putting her in her car seat for the first time. We left holding only the bag Max had packed for me. I gulped as I watched a new mom smiling down at her baby as she handed him to his father to be put in the car. Tears started to fill my eyes and the overwhelming feeling of loneliness crept inside me.

"Come on, Emma. Get inside the car." I slid inside and wiped the tear that fell from my eye. Max took hold of my hand and kissed the side of my head without saying a word.

I stepped inside my apartment first while Max followed behind with my bag and Darren carried up the flowers. I walked straight to the nursery and looked at the empty crib that was waiting for Sarah.

"It wasn't supposed to be this way. I was supposed to bring her home and show her how beautiful her room is." I wiped another tear that fell.

"I know, sweetheart, but you will be bringing her home and we need to be thankful for that."

"Every new mother is supposed to bring her baby home. Not leave her alone in a hospital!" I yelled.

"She's not alone, Emma. She's being well taken care of and looked after." He lightly gripped my shoulders and I jerked away from him.

"I'm her mother. She's supposed to be with me! With me." I began to cry.

Max cautiously wrapped his arms around me and pulled me into him, holding my head tightly against his firm chest as I continued to sob. We both slowly fell to the ground and he continued to hold me without saying a word. Once I calmed down, Max told me he had something for me. He got up and said that he'd be right back. A few moments later, he walked back in the room and handed me a long, velvet red box with gold trim. I slowly opened the lid, and inside sat a silver bracelet with three dainty silver charms. One of the charms was round and had a baby's footprint and Sarah's name engraved underneath. The other round charm said "Mom" and the third charm was of a beautiful silver butterfly.

"Max, it's beautiful."

"Do you really like it?"

"I love it. But you didn't have to do this."

"You're right. I didn't have to. I wanted to." He smiled.

He took the bracelet out of the box and placed it around my wrist. I looked up at him as he softly wiped away my tears and placed his hands on either side of my face. "We're in this together, Emma. You don't have to do it alone. I'll be there every step of the way. I know you don't want to hear this right now, but I came back for you because I love you. I'm so madly in love with you and being away for five months drove me insane. I'm here for you whether you want me to be or not."

I wrapped my arms around him and hugged him, burying my face in his neck. I didn't know where this was going and I was scared. So scared that I couldn't even tell him that I loved him too.

"Why did you leave me?" I blurted out unexpectedly.

"Because at the time, I thought it was the right thing to do. I was trying to save you from me. I was scared, Emma; frightened of my feelings for you. I was confused and unsure. I was so focused on getting out of New York and getting out from under my father's control, I couldn't see straight. Had I known you were pregnant, I never would have left. Did you know you were pregnant?"

"No. I didn't find out until a week later, the night your father paid me a visit."

He broke our embrace and looked at me. "What? He came here?"

"Yes. We got into it and he grabbed my arm and called me a filthy whore."

"WHAT?!" he shouted and I flinched. "He put his hands on you?"

"I found out I was pregnant that night after he left. I started having really bad cramping and Kara took me to the hospital. I thought it was appendicitis because I had been sick prior to that. It was when the doctor did an ultrasound that I found out."

Max got up. "I need to leave for a while, but I'll be back. Go lie down and get some rest."

"Max, no. Don't confront him."

"I have to, Emma. He won't get away with this. He had no right." He walked out of the room and out of my apartment.

****

Max

The rage I felt inside me was unlike anything I'd ever felt before. How dare that man harass Emma like he did. I took a cab over to my parents' house and called Darren to meet me there and wait outside. I ran up the steps and threw open the door. My mom came running down the stairs.

"Max. What the hell is going on?"

"Where is he?!" I yelled.

"Who?"

"Bradshaw. Who else?"

"What the hell are you doing here?" my father asked as he stepped into the living room.

Just the mere sight of him made me sick. I lunged at him and threw a punch, hitting him hard as he went down.

"Oh my God, Max. Stop!" My mom grabbed my arm and tried to hold me back.

"Did he tell you, Mom? Did he tell you how he went over to Emma's apartment and grabbed her arms, calling her a filthy whore?"

"What? Bradshaw, did you do that?"

He lay there on the ground, holding his jaw. "Yes. I did."

"Why?" my mom asked in anger.

"Because she wouldn't cooperate and tell me the truth."

"You son-of-a-bitch." I lunged at him again and grabbed him by the shirt. "Don't you ever fucking go near her again. After you left, she had to go to the hospital for severe stomach pains due to the stress you caused her. You know what she found out? That she was pregnant with my child."

My mom placed her hand over her mouth and lightly touched my arm. I jerked away from her.

"Don't you dare touch me," I snapped at her. "A few days ago, Emma gave birth to our baby, two months early, and now my daughter is fighting for her life in the NICU."

"A girl? I have a granddaughter?" She started to cry.

"No. You have nothing because you will never ever meet her and she will never know that the two of you exist."

"You can't do that," my father spoke.

I sharply turned towards him and saw the fear in his eyes. "You're no father. You're nothing but a filthy rich depressed man who's so unhappy with his life that you have to go and fuck every young woman you can get your hands on."

"Max! That's enough!" my mom screamed.

"Turn the other cheek, Mom. Because God knows you're so damn good at it. Stay by his side all you want. You both are dead to me and I will never raise my child in a home like I was raised in."

I stormed out of the living room and my mom ran after me, grabbing hold of my arm.

"Don't go. You're obviously upset and hurting. Let's talk about this and about your daughter."

"No. I tried to talk to you for years and you always took his side. Well, now you can be alone with him because you no longer have a son and I suspect, before too long, you won't have a daughter either. How does it feel to lose both your children?"

I opened the door and walked out as my mom screamed my name from the doorway. I hopped in the front seat of the Rolls Royce and told Darren to pull away immediately.

"I'm sorry, Max."

"It's fine, Darren. I've said what I came to say and now I'm going back to Emma. I have my company and my own family to focus on. I told her that I loved her today."

"How did she respond?"

"She didn't." I sighed. "I'm just going to wait for her for as long as it takes and I pray to God she still loves me."

****

Emma

I heard the door open as I lay on the couch. I sat up and looked at Max as he walked towards me.

"Are you okay?" I asked as he sat down next to me.

"I'm fine. I said what needed to be said and I told them about Sarah, but also that they will never meet her."

"Max."

"No, Emma. Don't. I don't want to think or talk about them. They no longer exist in my life. The only thing that matters to me is you and Sarah." He put his arm around me and pulled me into him, kissing the top of my head. "How are you feeling?"

"Okay, I guess. I can't stop thinking about Sarah and I want to see her so badly."

"I know. Me too. We'll see her first thing tomorrow morning."

There was silence for a while before I decided to bring something up. "I never talked to you about how I felt before we called off the engagement."

"What do you mean?"

"I never told you how I felt about you. I never told you that I was falling in love with you because I was scared that you didn't feel the same way and I didn't want you to feel guilty. Maybe I should have told you, but you were so excited about going to Chicago and starting your own business and I didn't want to ruin that for you. It was your opportunity to shine and I wasn't going to take that away. But when you left, I hated you for leaving me, even though you didn't know how I felt."

"But I knew, Emma. I knew you were in love with me. Why do you think I wrote you that letter? I swear to you I never meant to hurt you and the more time I spent away from you, the more I drank to get you off my mind, until one day I couldn't take it anymore. I missed everything about you. I missed your smile, your cute laugh, the way you smelled, kissing your beautiful lips, and waking up to your body wrapped around mine. You had dreams here in New York and I couldn't risk you losing them for someone like me. I would never ask you to give up your dream of going to Parsons. When I finally came back home and saw you were pregnant, the worst feeling in the world washed over me. I was so scared that she wasn't mine. If you're scared that I'll become my father, you don't have to be. I would never do that."

I needed to ask him a question, but I was too scared to know the truth, if he would even tell me the truth. I took in a deep breath.

"Did you sleep with anyone while you were in Chicago?"

"No," he replied without hesitation. "I didn't want anyone else. Only you."

"You're a guy and guys have needs."

"Yes, I do have needs and it wasn't a problem every time I looked at your picture, and there may have been some porn involved." He winked.

I couldn't help but smile. I stared into his eyes as he stared back. I stared so hard that I could see his soul. His beautiful, apologetic soul.

"I love you, Emma."

"I love you too, Max. I never stopped."

"I'm going to kiss your soft lips that I've missed so badly."

"Please do because I've missed yours too."

He brought his lips to mine and softly kissed me. It felt good to touch him again and even better to be loved by him.

"Will you stay with me tonight?" I asked.

"I'm never leaving you again." He smiled.

"We can't have sex for at least six weeks." I pouted.

"I know, and I'm okay with that because as long as I can kiss your lips, hold your hand, and wrap my arms around you, I'm good and I can wait."

Chapter 29

The days went by slowly and the countdown was on until we were able to bring our baby home. I spent all my days sitting with Sarah, holding her, watching her stare at me and wrapping her tiny hand around my finger. It had been four weeks since I delivered her and every day she was getting stronger. She was no longer in the incubator because her body was able to regulate its own temperature, which meant she was in an open crib where I had more access to her. She was my tiny miracle and I loved her so much. I didn't think it was possible to love someone so much. She had gained approximately two pounds since her birth, putting her at four pounds. She was thriving and I couldn't wait to bring her home. Unfortunately, that was not going to happen for about two to three more weeks. As I was holding her and trying to feed her, Max walked in.

"How are my girls?" he asked as he kissed my cheek.

"We're doing great. She's having a good day." I smiled.

Since I had been there all day with her, I got up from the chair and carefully handed her to Max. It was his turn to spend some time with his daughter. His company was taking off better than he expected and he spent most days at the office, but he always came to the hospital midday and at night. Since the girls couldn't visit Sarah, they would come to the hospital and we'd have lunch together and catch up.

"Guess what?" I said to Max.

"What?"

"I didn't tell you this earlier because I wanted to wait. I had my post-baby checkup today and I received the okay."

His eyes widened. "Are you sure?"

"Yes, and there's something else."

"What?"

"I want to go out on a date tonight."

"Just the two of us?" he asked.

"Did you want anyone else to go?" I laughed.

"No. I mean. God. I don't know what I mean." He smiled. "Of course we can go out on a date. Are you sure you're up to it?"

"The question is, Mr. Hamilton, are you up to it?" I winked.

"Emma, don't. I'm holding our daughter."

As soon as she was finished eating, we kissed her goodbye and went home to change and go on our date. Max had been staying at my place every night. I'd longed to make love to him. My longing had gotten so bad, I started dreaming about it. Thank God he never noticed. I took care of him every now and again and he was happy with that. But tonight, tonight was going to be the night that our bodies would connect again and become one.

"You look so beautiful." He smiled as he stared at me in my fitted black low cut dress and my black heels.

"Thank you. Can you put this on, please?" I handed him the butterfly necklace he gave me.

After putting it around me, he leaned in and planted tiny light kisses on my neck.

"Sorry, Mr. Hamilton, you'll have to wait until later."

"I'm just sampling." He smiled.

We left the apartment and had dinner at Per Se. As we were eating, Max stunned me with what he said.

"I have a proposed deal for you."

I cocked my head and slyly smiled at him. "What kind of deal?"

"I found a new apartment today and I need you and Sarah to move in with me, but I promise it's only for a specific amount of time."

"Really? And how much time are we talking?" I asked.

"Forever." He smiled.

"Hmm. If I do that for you, what's in it for me?"

"Me, of course. For a lifetime." He winked.

"I think that's a fair deal. Where's this apartment at?"

"I'll take you there tomorrow." He reached across the table and took my hand. "Listen, Emma. I want us both to start somewhere new. I could have easily asked you to move into my place, but since we're starting fresh and with Sarah, I thought it would be best to move. If you like the penthouse, then I would hire decorators to paint the nursery exactly how you already have it. Nothing would be changed."

"Penthouse? I like that idea, Max. I can't wait to see it."

"Good. I was hoping you'd be excited about it. We can go tomorrow morning before heading to the hospital."

After we finished eating, Max held his arm out and I took hold of it as we walked out of the restaurant.

"Where to now?" he asked.

"Home." I smiled.

"I was hoping you'd say that." He kissed my lips.

****

His hands swept over my body as if he had never touched me before. Slowly unzipping the back of my dress, Max pressed his lips against mine and took down each strap, letting it fall to the ground. My hand traveled to the front of him, feeling his already hard cock through the fabric of his pants. He moaned as my fingers deftly moved up and down him. He laid me down gently on the bed and hooked his fingers on each side of my panties, sliding them down and removing them. Unbuttoning his pants and sliding them off his hips, he climbed on the bed in between my legs as his tongue slowly slid up the inside of my thigh. I was already pulsating for him. I missed him so much and I missed his erotic touches. He set my body on fire with each flick of his tongue against my clit. When he slipped his finger inside of me, we both gasped. His mouth made its way up my torso, over my breasts, and up to my mouth, where his lips passionately kissed me as he manipulated my insides.

"I need to be inside of you now, Emma. I can't wait any longer. It's been far too long."

He grabbed hold of his manhood and slowly entered me. He was gentle and passionate and taking his time, savoring every moment with each long, deep thrust. I threw my head back in pleasure and wrapped my arms around him, pulling his naked body down onto mine.

"I love you so much," he whispered as his lips explored my neck.

"I love you too," I panted as his thrusts became faster and brought me to climax.

"You feel so good, baby. God, I've wanted you for so long."

He moved faster in and out of me, his cock swelling with delight as he thrust one last time, pulling out and releasing himself all over my stomach. He looked at me and smiled as he softly kissed my lips.

"I'll be right back."

He walked into the bathroom to grab some tissues as I lay there in my happy place, my body relaxed and the burning desire to fuck him again, but confused as to why he pulled out instead of coming inside of me. Max climbed in bed and wrapped his arms around me, pulling me close.

"Okay, we need to talk."

"About what?" he asked.

"Why didn't you come in me?"

He chuckled. "I'm sorry, but I got scared."

I laughed. "Scared of what?"

"That you'd get pregnant again."

"Well, I've been back on the pill for three weeks, but you're right. Now I'm a little nervous. Maybe we should get some latex-free condoms to use for the next couple of weeks or so. Just in case."

"We could or maybe I can just keep pulling out until we're one hundred percent sure it's safe. I have a feeling we'll be going through way too many condoms too fast because I plan on making love to you at least three times a day. We have a lot of catching up to do."

"We sure do, Mr. Hamilton, and I think I'm ready for round two."

"I love it when you say things like that." He smiled as he pulled me on top of him.

Chapter 30

Max and I got up bright and early the next morning. After showering together, we got dressed and headed to the penthouse that Max was dying to show me.

"So where exactly is this penthouse?" I asked as I took hold of his hand when he slid in next to me.

"East 61st Street. About eleven minutes from my other apartment. It's closer to my office and only one minute further to Parsons for you."

Darren pulled up to the curb and Max slid out, holding out his hand to me. I looked up and saw the name Trump Towers splayed across the front of the thirty-nine-story building. I gasped.

"This is Trump Towers."

"I know." Max chuckled. "Wait until you see the penthouse."

We took the elevator up to the thirty-second floor to apartment 32BC. When Max opened the door, an older lady approached us.

"Good morning, Mr. Hamilton."

"Good morning, Maggie. I'd like you to meet my girlfriend, Emma Knight."

"It's nice to meet you." She smiled as she held out her hand. "Let's take a look around, shall we?"

Just stepping through the front door, I already knew this was the perfect place for the three of us.

"This penthouse offers three bedrooms and four bathrooms, a separate den, and two private wraparound terraces. But the best part of this home is the views of Central Park from every room."

I was blown away by the elegance of the light stained oak flooring and the over-sized picture windows throughout the entire place.

"Let's start in the kitchen area. You can see this is a chef's kitchen with a pristine window over the sink, white stone countertops and top-of-the-line appliances by Miele, Wolf, and

Subzero. I can envision you cooking many wonderful meals here."

I looked at Max and he smiled because he knew all too well that I wasn't all that great of a cook.

"This is the dining area, which will seat eight people comfortably. Next, we have the large living area, which features one of the generous wraparound terraces, which faces the west, a beautiful feature for when you throw elegant parties. Next, we'll move onto the master suite, which features a private den off the back as well as the second wraparound private terrace. The best feature of this room is his and her bathrooms because we ladies know we need our own bathroom to accommodate all of our beauty products."

I stepped into the extremely large oversized walk-in closet and swallowed hard. I'd never seen anything like it. It was triple the size of the one I had at my apartment.

"Nice, isn't it?" Maggie smiled. "Now, if you open this door right here, it leads to the second walk-in closet for Mr. Hamilton. That way, you don't have to worry about space for your collection of clothes, shoes, jewelry, and handbags," she whispered.

"Max has more clothes and shoes than I have." I laughed.

"Not for long, sweetheart." He winked.

We stepped out of the room and into the hallway, where Maggie showed us the additional two guestrooms, each having their own bathroom.

"Well, what do you think?" Maggie asked.

"I love it. I'm speechless at how amazing this place is." I looked over at Max and placed my arm around his waist. "I can totally see us living here and making it our home."

"So you love it?" he asked.

"Yes. It goes beyond love."

He let out a sign of relief. "Thank God because I already bought it."

"What? When?" I laughed.

"Yesterday. I knew you'd love it and I was afraid it would sell before you had the chance to see it."

"I do love it, Max. Thank you." I reached up and gave him a kiss on his lips.

"You're welcome. I think the three of us will be very happy here."

"Congratulations to the both of you. You've made the right decision." Maggie smiled as she walked away.

"Yeah, of course we did because now she gets a huge commission," Max whispered in my ear.

"We'll need to go furniture shopping," I said. "Unless you just want to bring your furniture from your apartment."

"Nah. If we're starting new, then everything is going to be new and I want us to pick out furniture we both like together. Especially our bedroom set." He winked. "The only furniture coming here will be Sarah's from her nursery and I've already hired the decorators to duplicate the room."

"Have I told you how much I love you?" I asked with a smile.

"Not today, you haven't."

We stopped in front of the doorway and I wrapped my arms around his neck. "I love you to the moon and back, Mr. Hamilton."

"I love you more, Miss Knight. Now let's go see our baby girl."

****

After scrubbing up and stepping inside the NICU, Max and I walked over to Sarah. She was awake.

"There's my baby girl." I smiled as I picked up her tiny body and cradled her in my arms. "She looks so good, Max."

"Yes, she does." He bent down and kissed her head.

"Good news." Laney the nurse walked over and said with a huge smile. "You will get to take Sarah home in one week."

"Really?" Excitement overtook me. There was finally light at the end of the tunnel for us.

"Yep. She's doing better every day and getting stronger. She's drinking full bottles now and she's holding her own. Dr. Cooper will talk to you later when he gets here."

"Oh my God, Max. We'll finally get to bring her home. I'm so excited."

"Me too, baby. That means we have exactly one week to move and get everything in order."

"It's not possible," I said as I looked at him.

"Sure it is. We can do it. If you'll excuse me, I have several phone calls to make."

I smiled as he kissed me and walked out.

"Did you hear that, Sarah? You get to come home with Mommy and Daddy in one week." I smiled as I kissed her head and cuddled her against my chest.

We spent the next day traveling from furniture store to furniture store, picking out every piece of furniture we needed.

I had the best ideas of how to decorate and Max agreed with me.

"You're the interior designer, so anything you pick out will be amazing."

"Not an interior designer yet, my love."

"Well, consider our home your first project."

We picked out everything we needed to fill our space while the movers were at both my apartment and Max's, packing everything up. Max had to pull some strings to get the furniture delivered within a couple of days. Things were moving so fast that it was making my head spin. The nursery was being painted and the furniture was being moved over to the penthouse. I had given the colors to the painters to ensure they bought the right color paint.

It was now day six and tomorrow was the big day. Sarah was coming home. We spent our first night at our new place last night and christened our new bed more than once. Furniture wise, everything was in its place, including the nursery and all of Sarah's things I had purchased. Cardboard boxes filled most of the wall space with our things in them from the other apartments and I had planned to start unpacking after I went to the hospital to visit Sarah. It was a Saturday and Max told me he had to stop by the office for a bit to catch up on some work and that he'd meet me at the hospital.

As I was feeding Sarah her bottle and rocking her in the chair, Max walked in with a big smile on his face.

"Hi." He bent down and gave us both a kiss.

"Hi. Did you get some work done?"

"I sure did. Let's go to lunch. I'm starving."

"Okay. We can grab something to eat in the cafeteria."

"Emma, I was thinking of a nice restaurant. Aren't you sick of eating this hospital food?"

"A little, but I don't want to leave her."

He gave me a small smile as he knelt down beside me. "We'll come back later and she'll be home tomorrow."

"Okay."

After I fed her, Max took her from me and burped her. Watching him with her was one of the most precious moments of my life. He was a natural and he loved her more than anything in the world. After we laid her down and said goodbye, Max took me to a place called Anassa Taverna.

"What restaurant is this?" I asked as we stepped out of the Rolls Royce.

"A place with really good food." He smiled.

We walked through the large doors and Max led me up the stairs. When I reached the top step, everyone yelled, "Surprise!" I was taken back as I placed my hand over chest.

"Oh my God. What is this?" I asked in excitement as I looked around at all the people staring at me.

"It's your baby shower!" Molly exclaimed as she hugged me.

I looked at Max and he had a big grin on his face. "Did you do this?"

"I helped." He winked.

I looked around at the tables that were covered in white tablecloths with a light pink overlay. White and pink balloons with Sarah's name were scattered everywhere and centerpieces made of white and pink roses filled each table. Tears sprang to my eyes as Kara and Aubrey hugged me.

"You didn't think we'd let you go without a shower, did you?"

"I didn't think about it, actually."

I was overwhelmed and overjoyed. "I have another surprise for you." Max smiled as he took my hand and led me over to the corner of the bar, where I saw my mom and Danny sitting.

I could no longer hold back the tears as she walked over to me and gave me a hug.

"Oh, my baby girl. I've missed you so much."

"Mom. I'm so happy you're here. I can't wait for you to meet Sarah."

"You look amazing, Emma." Danny smiled as he hugged me.

"When did you two get in?" I asked.

"Last night. Thanks to Max here." She placed her hand on his chest. "Oh my." She smiled.

I let out a laugh and then walked around to the hundred guests that had attended. A majority were Max's friends and coworkers and my friends from school.

"Fiona wished she could be here, but she's in the middle of a job in Paris and couldn't fly out."

"She couldn't get out, but I could!" I heard a familiar voice behind me.

"Macy!" I turned and hugged her.

"Congratulations, Emma. I'm so happy for you and Max."

"Thank you."

I spent some time talking to Hannah and Austin before it was time to sit down and eat. Max sat beside me and took hold of my hand.

"Are you happy?"

"Incredibly. Thank you so much for this, Max. I think I'll keep you around." I winked.

"I hope so." He brushed his lips against mine.

After I opened the mounds of presents ranging from baby books, toys, equipment, and clothes, everyone was beginning to leave.

"How are we going to get all this stuff home?" I asked.

"I have a truck outside, waiting for my signal to come up and start loading."

"You think of everything, Mr. Hamilton."

"I try, Miss Knight."

I was excited to get home and show the girls and my mom our new home. As soon as we walked through the doors, everyone gasped.

"Holy shit! Look at this place!" Molly exclaimed.

"Absolutely stunning," Kara chimed.

"Oh, Emma, this is gorgeous," my mom said with tears in her eyes. She took hold of my hands. "You are so lucky to have Max in your life. He's a good man, Emma. He's got a heart of gold. I can tell."

"Where did he put you up at?" I asked with a smile.

"The Trump Hotel."

"And what a hell of a hotel it is," Danny spoke.

Max laughed as he wrapped his arms around my waist from behind. "I'm happy you like it there."

My mom put her arm around Danny and looked at both Max and me. "We have some news of our own. We're getting married!"

I put my hands over my mouth. "Mom! That's wonderful news. Congratulations." I hugged them both tightly. "When?"

"We decided to wait about six months. We're going to do it right with a wedding and all. I wanted to wait until it was safe for Sarah to travel and I want you to be my maid of honor."

Tears sprang to my eyes as I looked at her. "Of course I'll be your maid of honor," I squealed.

We spent the early evening talking and catching up. As soon as they left, Max and I went to the hospital to visit Sarah. We held her, played with her, talked to her, and gave her lots of little kisses. Our little bundle of joy was finally coming home tomorrow and we couldn't be happier.

Chapter 31

As Max and I walked out of the hospital with our baby girl, we finally looked like new parents. I had bought little gifts of thank you to give to all the nurses who took special care of her in the NICU. They had become like family to us. Being there every day, talking to them, and getting to know each of them personally, we felt that they had a special place in our hearts and we couldn't thank them enough for all they'd done for our little girl.

Stepping into our apartment, I was shocked when I walked in and the mess that consumed us between all the things from the baby shower and our move was suddenly gone.

"Max, what happened here?"

"I had people come in and organize everything. We couldn't bring our daughter home to a mess."

"That was so sweet of you. But how are we going to know where everything is?"

"You'll learn, baby. Don't sweat the small stuff." He winked.

We took Sarah to the nursery and laid her down in her crib. She stared up at us with her beautiful eyes and kicked her little legs.

"She likes her new bed." I smiled.

"Anything is better than what she was sleeping in all those weeks."

I gently smacked Max on the arm and laughed.

My mom and Danny came over that evening and when my mom saw Sarah, she started to cry.

"She's beautiful, Emma. She looks just like you."

"You think?"

"Yes. I do. I can see some of Max in her as well. You two make beautiful babies."

"We do, don't we?" Max said as he clasped my shoulders.

After visiting for a while, they left because they had an early flight back to Miami in the morning. I was sad to see her go but more than ready to be alone with Max and Sarah. The past months had been the hardest and it was going to be nice to finally start living a normal life again.

****

The first week was rough. Sarah only slept a couple hours each time, so she was up most of the night. When she awoke at three a.m., Max said that he'd feed her. I didn't argue because I was exhausted. As I lay there, I could hear him talking to her over the baby monitor.

"You are the most beautiful girl I've ever laid eyes on, well, except for your mommy. Since we're going to be here a while, Daddy has a story to tell you about butterflies."

I smiled as I listened to him tell her all about the butterflies. I got out of bed and stood in the doorway of the nursery.

"I'll always make sure you dance, princess. You will never have to worry about anything. Your life will be filled with love and happiness and no matter what obstacles you face, your mom and dad will always be here to make sure you get through it and continue to dance throughout your life."

I walked over to him and sat on the arm of the chair, placing my arm around his neck. When he looked up at me, I leaned down and softly kissed his lips. We both looked at Sarah, who was now fast asleep.

"I love you both so much," he said.

"We love you too, baby. More than anyone else in the entire world."

I carefully took her from his arms and laid her down in her crib. Max walked over and picked me up, carrying me to the bedroom.

"I need to make love to you right now. If that's okay."

"It's more than okay and believe me when I tell you that I'm more than ready for you."

He raised his eyebrow as he laid me down on the bed, pushing the edge of my panties to the side and feeling how wet I was for him.

"You sure are, my love." He smiled.

****

Another week had passed and it was a beautiful Sunday afternoon. Max was so excited to take Sarah for a walk to Central Park. He was all smiles as he put her in her new stroller.

"Look at how amazing this stroller is. Doesn't she look beautiful in it? Push it, Emma. Feel how smooth the ride is."

I couldn't help but laugh at him. He was like a kid with a new toy. As we were walking down the street, Max abruptly stopped. I didn't know why at first because I had my head turned, looking at some of the window displays. When I turned my head, I saw his mother standing in front of the stroller. He didn't say a word. He just glared at her.

"Carol," I spoke.

She looked down at Sarah and tears filled her eyes.

"Let's go, Emma," Max said sternly as he attempted to push the stroller.

"Max." I placed my hand on his arm. "Carol, this is your granddaughter, Sarah."

"She's beautiful. What a beautiful name. She's okay?"

"Yes. She's doing great. She's very healthy."

"Thank God." She sighed. "Max, we need to talk."

"I have nothing to say to you. Now if you'll excuse me, we have somewhere we need to be."

"I want to apologize to you for everything. I've left your father. Please say we can all have dinner and talk."

"It's too late for that. Now excuse us."

I looked at Carol and could feel her pain. "I'll talk to him," I whispered as I touched her arm."

We walked away. "Don't, Emma. Don't say a word. I'm not having this day with our daughter ruined. We'll talk about it later."

"Okay." He was hurting. I could tell and I respected him enough to wait and talk about it later.

We reached Central Park and headed over to the Alice in Wonderland statue.

"Go sit down on the mushroom with Sarah and I'll take your picture."

I smiled as I took her from her stroller and held her. As I sat on the mushroom, Max took our picture.

"Now you come join us for a selfie."

I scooted over and he sat down next to me, taking Sarah from my arms and holding her up so she was in the picture.

"Smile," I said as I took our picture a couple of times.

Max got up, and as he held Sarah, he bent down on one knee in front of me.

"What are you doing?"

He swallowed hard.

"Emma, I love you and Sarah so much that I never thought it could be possible. My love for you is so overwhelming that it makes me incredibly happy. You make me incredibly happy and I can't imagine life without you and Sarah. You've completed my entire world. Hell, you've completed my entire universe. You have brought so much good into my life and have taught me so many things. I need you and want you to be my forever. Will you do me the honor of becoming my wife?"

My teary eyes stared into his as my heart began racing. This was so unexpected and the fact that he proposed to me while holding our daughter made me the happiest woman in the world.

"Yes, Max, I will marry you!"

"Really?"

"Yes!" I smiled.

"Did you hear that, Sarah? Your mom said yes!"

He leaned over and kissed me passionately. "Here, take her for a second."

I took Sarah from him as he reached into his pants pocket and pulled out a beautiful diamond ring.

"This ring is a new one because we're starting over, and I never want you to take it off. It symbolizes my love for you and a new beginning. This isn't a proposed deal, Emma. It's the real thing and I wanted you to have something new. Not something that was a reminder of what the old ring represented. I hope you like it." He slipped the ring on my finger.

"It's beautiful and stunning. I love it." I smiled.

We both stood up and I put Sarah back in her stroller, then Max and I hugged tightly as he picked me up and spun me around. "I love you, Emma. More than words could ever say."

"I love you too, Max. I love you so much."

His lips locked with mine as we passionately kissed until Sarah decided to cry. We both laughed as we pushed her around Central Park, taking in the summer warmth and the beauty of nature that surrounded us.

Not all that long ago, Max Hamilton and I made a deal. A deal that neither one of us thought would change our lives forever. Fate stepped in that night we first met in Miami and led us on a journey that got us to where we were today. It wasn't an easy journey, but I wouldn't have traded it for the world. Max and Sarah were my entire life and I loved them both with my heart and soul.

We were married a year later. Sarah was my flower girl and looked like a princess as she walked down the aisle to her daddy. Darren walked me down the aisle and gave my hand to Max. As we stood there in front of our family and friends, we said our vows to each other while our daughter stood in front of us and watched. She had her moments, but it was all good. Max eventually reconciled with his mother, but not his father. The scars were too deep, and I couldn't really blame him. Fiona flew back from Paris to attend the wedding, and my mom and stepdad, Danny, also flew in. Max once again put them up at The Trump because he knew how much they loved it there.

I was now Mrs. Emma Hamilton and married to the love of my life. I never would have thought that the hot and sexy man I stared at across the bar at a nightclub in Miami would become my husband and that we'd have a beautiful healthy daughter. Max's proposed deal turned out to be the best deal of a lifetime and I couldn't image my life any other way.

BOOKS BY SANDI LYNN

The Forever Series:

Forever Black, Forever You, Forever Us, Being Julia

A Forever Christmas, Collin

A Millionaire's Love Series:

Lie Next To Me, When I Lie With You

Love Series:

Love In Between, The Upside of Love

A Love Called Simon

Stand Alones:

She Writes Love

Then You Happened

Remembering You (A Novella)

About The Author

Sandi Lynn is a *New York Times, USA Today* and *Wall Street Journal* bestselling author who spends all of her days writing. She published her first novel, *Forever Black*, in February 2013 and hasn't stopped writing since. Her addictions are shopping, romance novels, coffee, chocolate, margaritas, and giving readers an escape to another world.

Please come connect with her at:

www.facebook.com/Sandi.Lynn.Author

www.twitter.com/SandilynnWriter

www.authorsandilynn.com

www.pinterest.com/sandilynnWriter

www.instagram.com/sandilynnauthor

https://www.goodreads.com/author/show/6089757.Sandi_Lynn

Playlist

Fidelity ~ Jasmine Thompson

All of Me ~ Jasmine Thompson

Uptown Funk ~ Mark Ronson, Bruno Mars

Nothing Compares To U ~ Sinead O'Connor

What If You ~ Joshua Radin

It's You ~ Ryan Cabrera

Better Man ~ James Morrison

Goodbye My Lover ~ James Blunt

A Little Bit Stronger ~ Sara Evans

Printed in Great Britain
by Amazon.co.uk, Ltd.,
Marston Gate.